Praise for the first
BEN HENRY novel,
No Go on Jackson Street

"Strong, smart and a pleasure to read!"
Robert B. Parker

―――――――――

"Hard-boiled, snappy . . . refreshing"
Publishers Weekly

―――――――――

"In the best Dashiell Hammett tradition"
Booklist

ALL POINTS BULLETIN

MIKE WEISS

AVON BOOKS ◆ NEW YORK

ALL POINTS BULLETIN is an original publication of Avon Books. This work has never before appeared in book form. This work is a novel. Any similarity to actual persons or events is purely coincidental.

AVON BOOKS
A division of
The Hearst Corporation
105 Madison Avenue
New York, New York 10016

Copyright © 1989 by Michael Weiss
Published by arrangement with the author
Library of Congress Catalog Card Number: 88-92981
ISBN: 0-380-75715-X

First Avon Books Printing: September 1989

AVON TRADEMARK REG. U.S. PAT. OFF. AND IN OTHER COUNTRIES, MARCA REGISTRADA, HECHO EN U.S.A.

Printed in the U.S.A.

K-R 10 9 8 7 6 5 4 3 2 1

To Bruce and Audrey Conard

Bid them wash their faces,
And keep their teeth clean.

Coriolanus
Shakespeare

Prologue

The first murder—though at the time nobody knew it would become the first—warranted four column inches near the bottom of page 2 of The Courier beside the Brooks Brothers pre-Christmas ad. Perhaps the murder of a cab driver might have attracted more notice if the police had said that whoever had repeatedly stabbed Frank Iancini and then slit his throat from ear to ear had not taken any of the $112 he had on him. But they didn't.

Probably the only people in San Francisco who had not known Frank Iancini personally but who were nonetheless deeply affected by his death were the wives and lovers of cab drivers. Most every married driver in the city had a fight or a fuck when he got home on the day the story ran.

But the Iancini story disappeared almost immediately amid the preholiday festivity. So when Arnold Pachter was killed in a similar fashion during a rainstorm in the second week of February, nobody but a few cops in the Taxi Detail and the Homicide Squad made the connection. The cops, of course, didn't tell the newspapers. But taxi drivers don't need newspapers to tell them what's happening on their streets. What they didn't know could hurt them.

By five o'clock on the evening of the day Arnold Pachter died, several thousand San Francisco cab drivers were well and thoroughly frightened. Not Albert Dwiri, though. Albert had other things on his mind.

1

Albert's hemorrhoids were bothering him something awful and he was tired. But the bone-deep weariness was a condition he had ceased to notice years before. He was almost never not tired. Albert had been on the street for two hours, and now the sun was blinding, its fierce light bursting into an undifferentiated glare where it struck the greasy window of his cab. As far as Albert was concerned, this was the worst part of the day, when the sun was going down and the homebound traffic was clogging the streets. Soon the sun would set, and the dim evening would deliver him from the hellish light, but he was not anticipating that. It was the Mexican boy Angel Cortez who plagued his thoughts.

The filthy little greaser had pulled up Razor's Edge coming into the top of the stretch; anybody could see that the little bastard was throwing the race. The bay horse had been moving strongly along the rail, intent on overtaking the lone horse ahead of it, until Cortez had tightened the bit and hauled back on the reins. The fix was so clear an owl could have seen it in broad daylight. The stewards never blinked.

Albert had seen Cortez yank the straining, baffled horse off its pace, and the four $50 win tickets in his shirt pocket, the plunge that was going to change his run of bad luck and take care of his problem with Chris Manchuco, lost their radiant tingle, their Christmas-present excitement, and became one more disappointment. Albert should have known better. The bastards never gave you an even break.

Albert was angry, angry and scared at what Chris Manchuco might do when he didn't come up with the cash payment. But to look at his face you would not have known Albert was frightened. His skin was pasty, his forehead deeply lined, his rheumy eyes sunk in smudgy hollows. Albert's nose was long and thin, and though it was gray at its round tip, its length was festooned with burst capillaries. He looked fifty-five, maybe even sixty years old, but in fact was only forty-eight. Twenty-five years he had been driving, twenty-five years and the bastards never gave him an even break, not ever. The resignation in his worn face was complete. That filthy little greaser, he thought again, but without passion, submissively.

He twisted on the grimy plastic seat and tried to slip the fingers of his right hand down the back of his pants to scratch at his scalding itch. It was just at that moment that he saw the guy at the bus stop flagging down his taxi. He pulled his hand out of his pants, momentarily forgetting his itch, and pulled to the curb a short way past the flag. It had been a long time since Albert had bothered to look closely at who was getting into the back seat of his taxi. Certain elements you just didn't stop for. His sense for potential danger was so deeply ingrained that he had long ceased to think about it, except on those rare occasions when his inner alarm sounded a warning. Like his tiredness, Albert's wariness had become reflexive.

The passenger pulled the door closed behind him. Albert half turned toward him.

"Where ya headed?"

"How long to the city pier?" A dark shirt open at the collar. Black hair cut short. Albert watched the fare take out a folded pocket handkerchief, wipe off the discolored seat, and then slide over to sit on the place he had wiped.

"Traffic's bad going down there this time," Albert told him, indifferent to the load's having cleaned the seat, as indifferent as he was to the butts and ashes on the cab's floor, the gritty surfaces, the stains from coffee, human dirt, and God knew what else that streaked and blotched the tan upholstery. For Albert, a taxi was four wheels and a meter. "Even if it ain't, I don't break no speeding laws. That's a forty-buck ticket and a point on the license."

"I have to be there six-thirty. You know the way?"

"Yeah, sure," Albert said. He had already lost all interest in the load. He punched the meter and started to drive, the route he would take—down to Mission, Mission to Valencia, across Market to Franklin to Bay to Van Ness and onto the pier—appearing automatically in his mind. Those computerized route finders they were offering as options on expensive new cars, they were just catching up with Albert's mind.

Along Franklin traffic was thick and sluggish. Albert was thinking about a hot sitz bath, about sinking his ass down into nearly scalding water. Nothing better for the piles. He hoped Cortez had a hemorrhoid the size of a fist. What was the use? A lot Chris Manchuco would care about the crooked jockey. The bookie was a wise guy, just the one who would have been in the know about the fix. There were winners and there were losers, Albert thought; who knows why?

"Ever been down the St. Francis Hotel?" Albert asked.

"What?"

"The St. Francis. Down at Union Square, y'know?"

The fare said nothing.

"It don't probably matter none to you, but you know Al Jolson died playing gin rummy there, at the St. Francis. You know what I think? I tell ya. A guy with luck like him, he was holding crap when he checked out. You think a winner like that's gonna check out when he's holding the cards? No way. They never put it in the papers or nothing, what his hand was. But you can take it from me. Crap."

"Can't you take a way without so much traffic, driver?"

"What's your problem, bub? It's rush hour, like." Albert sneaked a quick look in the rearview. The fare was sitting in the middle of the seat, staring straight ahead. He didn't say anything more, so Albert thought maybe he didn't understand English real good. He looked like maybe he could be part Filipino or something. Tagalong, Albert thought; they got the goddamn gas station signs in Tagalong. Spanish and Chinese ain't enough, they need Tagalong, too. That's what the city was coming to, Tagalong on the gas pumps.

Well, if the guy had nothing to say except to blame him for the goddamn traffic, it was alright with Albert if he kept his mouth shut. That was just fine with Albert. When they had finally reached the sloping drive that led to the city pier where it jutted into the churning waters of the inner Golden Gate, the fare spoke again.

"Stop right here."

"Can't," Albert explained.

"You wait a minute. I want to get out and look around."

"Yeah, well, it's no problem waiting. But this here is a no-stopping zone. Cop over there is gonna hassle me if I wait." He pointed at the black-and-white about twenty yards up on the opposite side of the drive. *"They never give a taxi a break, ya know what I mean?"*

"Take me by Holly Park Circle."

"Holly Park Circle?" Albert glanced at the meter: $6.90. *"That's way back out by where I picked you up from, Holly Park. You want to go back out, huh?"* Albert considered asking to see the color of the fare's money, but it would probably cost him his tip if the guy was insulted. *"Sure thing,"* he said, and started back the way they had come. It was turning into a pretty good ride. Albert's spirits rose, but only marginally.

Traffic was bumper to bumper along Van Ness until he passed City Hall, and then he missed a couple of lights so it was dusk by the time they reached Holly Park. The load hadn't said anything on the ride back, and neither had Albert. He wanted to get this guy out of his cab so he could give his ass a proper scratching. Maybe he'd even stop by the Hub Pharmacy and pick up some of that Preparation H. It would hold him until his shift was over and he could sink into a sitz bath.

The load was mumbling something Albert couldn't make out. Something foreign-sounding. Tagalong, right? Albert looked at his load again in the rearview, and what he saw drained his face and hands of blood. The blood rushed to his pumping heart and made him cold. The guy had a long knife in his hand, and he was running a thumbnail along the blade edge as if to test its sharpness.

"Hey," Albert said.

"I've got to kill you now."

"Wait a goddamn minute," Albert said, half turning in his seat to look at the load in disbelief.

He saw the butcher knife plunging toward him and wet his pants. The blade was a vicious steel triangle. Albert screamed with fear, and instinctively reached for the knife, to ward it off. It was like television, something he was watching that had nothing to do with him. He reached for the knife, clutching at the blade, which was so sharp he didn't feel it when the index and middle fingers of his hand were severed. He had forgotten completely that the cab was still moving, and was thrown against the steering wheel by the impact when the car smashed into a lamppost. The jolt sent the man with the knife halfway over the front seat. Albert kept struggling, grasping for the knife. The terror was sending violent spasms through his intestines. The ferocity of his urge to survive kept him struggling despite his wounds and his being winded from the crash. It was the first time in Albert's life that he wanted something enough to fight desperately for it. He wanted to live.

Their faces were tight together. The bastard was breathing through his nose, short rapid breaths. He kept lifting the knife and plunging it toward Albert. Albert grabbed for the blade and punched out for what seemed like a very long time, until finally he felt the strength oozing out of his body. He was starting to grow dizzy and a blackness was creeping over his eyes, starting at the outside corners. The cop car, Albert thought; that's why he didn't do it at the pier. He held onto that thought because he knew that when the blackness got all the way across, he would stop thinking and die.

"Please," he said. "Please. I don't want to die."

The bastard's forehead jammed tight against his own. Albert tried to move his head back so he could meet his eyes, but it was impossibly difficult. The last thing Albert saw was the knife being held in front of his face, like the bastard wanted him to see it.

Albert cried, "I'm sorry, Ma."

One

Seymour Lloyd was the only guy I ever knew to die from flossing his teeth. Coming across the news of his death at the back of the paper, I tilted the boiling kettle too suddenly over the grounds, and little coffee missiles took off and exploded all over the clean stovetop and the white wall. I reached for a sheet of paper towel. It had been a long night, one of those nights when the pillow is hard as a headstone, and I had been tossed and turned by dismaying and lurid self-assessments. Now the sun was up, a long and empty day awaited me, and Seymour Lloyd was dead.

I began my day by wiping coffee stains off the wall and nagging myself to buy another roll of paper towels—the one in the holder was half used and there wasn't a backup roll in the house. I hardly knew Seymour, who had been a bail bondsman with a storefront office across from the Hall of Justice. His name was painted on the plate-glass window in gold gilt, and the afternoon sun was kept out by closing the extra-long green venetian blinds. In the course of one thing and another I had talked with him a few times and found him to be not only extravagantly admiring of himself but rude to a fault. About all I could find to say in his favor was that he did not wear a diamond pinkie ring.

So on a Monday morning a few months back when I had had nothing better to do, I had decided to tail him. It was an educational project. Somebody in my new line of work was meant to know how to tail a person, though how I was supposed to learn besides watching Humphrey Bogart movies was a mystery to me. The one thing I was certain of was that I couldn't ask a plainclothes cop or any of the private investigators I knew, not if I wanted to show my face anywhere ever again. So I decided to make Seymour's life my practice course.

By Wednesday I knew that Seymour's routine held all the fascination of a lint ball. He left his house at the same time each weekday morning, and his wife came out on the steps with him in a faded rose-colored wrap to retrieve the newspaper. Seymour bought his own paper at the mom-and-pop where he got the day's bets down. He was at his office, or across the street at the Hall attending to business, every morning until twelve-thirty, when he drove to The Cargo restaurant on Third Street, a hangout favored by the Hall of Justice crowd. He had the tartar steak with capers and Vinnie's salad. Used Sweet 'n Low in his coffee.

After lunch he got back into his big Buick with the personalized license plates BAIL, and went around and popped his girlfriend before returning to the office. On the way from The Cargo to see the girl—her specialty at the O'Farrell Street club where she danced was riding a velveteen sawhorse— Seymour flossed.

I dampened the wadded-up paper towel and went on the attack against the coffee stains. The towel was manufactured by Scott and cost a couple of pennies more but held up best when damp. When I had wiped out the stains I tossed the towel into the bin. The bin was almost full. I tied off the white plastic garbage bag, put it aside for disposal, and got a fresh one from the cabinet. While the coffee dripped I did a little light sweeping. Unlike Seymour's, my own life as a foot soldier in the never-ending battle against household shmutz was a tale of breathtaking variety and excitement.

The best part of tailing Seymour had been when we were

both in our cars. Like all taxi drivers, active and retired, I knew nobody could drive the city the way I could. The other 100 million Americans who feel the same way about their own driving are wrong. So as Seymour maneuvered his black Riviera with the red plush seats through traffic, I buzzed around him like a cowboy herding doggies. Mostly I stayed somewhere behind him, but a few times I moved up into the blind zones on his left or right bumpers, and once I had upped the ante by passing him and arriving outside the girl's hotel before him. While he paid his visit I waited in my car thinking that this new gig of mine was a hell of an improvement on the old one. I mean, I used to be a mere taxi driver, a slave to a meter. Now I ran around burning up my own gas and *nobody* paid me for it. Did I have a leg up or what?

Anyway, that's how I knew Seymour Lloyd flossed his teeth every day between one-twenty when he left The Cargo and one-thirty when he parked behind the Crystal Hotel on Fourth Street and took the elevator to room 303. Of course, yesterday he never arrived. I felt sorry for the girl. She probably hadn't known why Seymour didn't show until she read about it in the newspaper.

No doubt Seymour had been flossing as usual when he bumped across the Southern Pacific tracks and came up on the entrance to the Greyhound yard on Seventh Street, near Daggett; if he hadn't been flossing he might be alive today. The Greyhound drivers are real cowboys, and one of them wheeled a big interstate out of the yard and onto Seventh Street as if that stretch of asphalt belonged exclusively to him. Sic transit Seymour.

The cool morning air felt tingly against my freshly shaved cheeks. It was early and the pale light cast by the springtime sun as it rose behind the Bay Bridge painted the North Beach streets, damp with lingering fog, in soft hues. The infant day was a watercolor. Like most half-truths, it was alluring.

Something was disturbing Gino, I saw that as soon as I

took a stool at his counter. His place smelled of fried grease, coffee, cigarettes, and newsprint. While Gino took my order he was staring angrily at the only other customer, a skinny kid methodically downing a tall stack of pancakes awash in syrup and butter.

"Hey, that's a nice T-shirt," Gino told him while he poured my coffee.

"This?" The kid looked down at his concave chest, his long hair falling over his eyes, and smirked knowingly. Pink blemishes still dusted his long chin, and there were roses blooming in his cheeks. The tight-fitting T-shirt was black, and written across his chest in white letters were the words "Stamp Out Virgins."

"I never seen one like it," Gino said.

"I got it over the head shop up on Market Street." There was a sly pride in the kid's eyes. I sat back to watch Gino blindside him while pretending to read my paper.

"T-shirts," Gino said. "I don't know, you wear them what, a year maybe, they get holes. They make 'em cheap. See?" He stuck a thick index finger into a hole the size of a half dollar in his red 49ers T-shirt, and wiggled it comically. "This one you got on, you shouldn't throw it away, it's special, you know? When it gets old, holes, you should hold onto it. A memento, like. You a student, right?"

"I'm accepted at State."

"That's good. I can see you got a future. Okay, you graduate, right, you still got your T-shirt, you save it way at the back of your bottom drawer. So someday you meet a nice college girl, you settle down, and before you know it, bam," Gino said, slamming his palms, "babies. They look just like their mother, beautiful. Like my own girls. Four I got, oldest about your age. A good girl. She's going to college, too, secretarial."

"Really?" the boy said. He had cleaned his plate and was bored and confused by Gino. "That must be interesting."

"Daughters," Gino said, shaking his head musingly. "One

day, my God, so soon, a young man comes around. Okay. Now. This is where you go way into the back of the drawer, this shirt you almost forgot you got.'' Gino pantomimed taking out the shirt and holding it up for inspection. ''You ask yourself, how do you feel if this boy out there in the living room waiting for your beautiful young daughter is wearing a T-shirt like this?'' Gino gave the boy a hard smile.

The kid didn't know what to do with his eyes. His cheeks turned red and his fingers crept down the front of his windbreaker zipper, then slid into his pockets. He stood up to leave, not sure whether or not he should be smiling. He was careful to close the door quietly after he had paid and left.

I said to Gino, ''You only got the one worthless son.''

He started laughing so hard he had to double over, and when he tried to talk only wheezes came out. ''Can't . . . a . . . man . . . oh, jeez . . . dream?''

Just as I was pulling the sports section loose, the door opened again and a loud, cheerful contralto sang out, ''Your taxi's here, mister.''

I swung around on my stool. ''Frieda!''

''You look hungry,'' Gino said, still wiping tears of mirth off his stubbly cheeks.

She laughed, an explosive guffaw that began in the diaphragm. Frieda Mishkin was an underemployed diva, and she always looked hungry. She nearly filled the width of the doorway. There was a woven bag slung over the shoulder of her denim jacket, and her floral peasant blouse bulged with flesh. She wore pointy-toed, ankle-high black leather lace-ups that were neither Victorian nor Marine combat boots but owed something to each. Her taxi, Checker 509, was parked in the bus zone outside.

Frieda gave me a quick buss on the cheek. Almost involuntarily I sniffed her perfume. There was a tiny gap between her two front teeth, which boyhood folklore held was the sign of a passionate nature. She hoisted herself onto the stool beside mine, her buttocks in a denim skirt overflowing it.

"Eyes above the waist, darlin'. Is the coffee in here safe to drink?"

"Hey!" Gino said, as I said, "No."

"I already ate anyway," Frieda told Gino. "How about a couple of chocolate doughnuts and a cuppa." She shifted her attention to me. "Staying out of trouble?"

"I've been tailing a guy," I said. "And I've got a couple of other things cooking." Potatoes and fried eggs, just to mention two.

"You hear about the new medallions?"

I shook my head to show I hadn't.

"Right. Madam our Mayor wants three hundred new medallions on the street for the convention." The Democrats were coming to San Francisco to nominate a candidate who would get his brains kicked in in November by Reagan, thereby earning the undying enmity of a grateful party. "That's a forty percent increase in the number of cabs on the street, forty percent out of my pocket. Every driver's pocket." She was already working on her second doughnut.

"Wait just a minute here," I said. "You aren't suggesting, are you, that our mayor puts her own ambitions in front of the economic well-being of taxi drivers? I can hardly believe what I'm hearing. Doesn't Abigail herself tell us that what's best for San Franciscans is her last thought at night and her first in the morning?"

"Right," Frieda said. "Like, what's white and twelve inches long?"

"I give up."

"Nothing!"

When I had stopped laughing, Frieda said, "Okay, there's this broad from Los Angeles named Sally something or other, Sally Bender, in charge of convention arrangements and she's up here staying at the Palace. It's rush hour, right? Five o'clock on a Friday, it's raining, and she's looking for a taxi. Good luck. The poor thing gets soaked. She just happens to tell her good friend Abigail how hard it is to find a taxi in San Francisco when you need one. So what does Madam do?"

"Calls her husband?"

Frieda fixed me with a disapproving stare. "Just because she's a pussy doesn't mean you can get away with being a sexist."

I thought of my crisply made bed, the clean stovetop, the Scott towels I had to remember to pick up. I thought of my ex-wife and how I felt now about Jessica Gage. I said not a word. Gino slid my breakfast in front of me, and I busied myself eating while he refilled both our cups.

"Right. Abigail's pushing for three hundred new medallions so Sally what's-her-face and her friends won't go around saying Abigail's not a hands-on mayor after all. But she's not going to get away with it. We're going to stop her cold."

"We?"

Frieda pointed a stubby index finger with deep creases at the knuckle toward a brown-and-white campaign button on her denim jacket. "The Alliance."

"Alliance? Give me a break, Frieda. You couldn't get two drivers to agree on the shortest route from First to Second Street, let alone to an effective labor action."

"Minna Alley," Frieda said. "No lights."

"Howard Street, honey. No intersection in between."

"For how much?" Frieda brayed and slapped me across the back. She leaned closer, conspiratorially, and put her hand, palm down, just above my knee. I could hardly concentrate on what she was saying next, so uncomfortable did the presence of her hand on my leg make me feel. I fought to keep my discomfort from showing in my face. When I tuned back in she was saying something about a taxi strike, if it came to that.

"I don't know, Frieda. There are only two things in this world that make our mayor's little light burn brightly. One is her own ambition for power. Abigail thinks she's got a shot at being the first Vice Presidential nominee of a major political party. The other is order. Frieda, doll, before you go up against her with only a bunch of drivers frightened of losing their jobs, you better check out what that other order freak, Mussolini, did to the anarchists." I had no idea whether Mussolini had done anything to the anarchists, but it had just popped out and I doubted Frieda knew either.

She lifted her hand off my leg and pressed her index finger on her plate, lifting off crumbs and licking them. "The objective conditions are changing," she said seriously. "Madam's got the drivers scared for their jobs, and these killings have them shit scared altogether."

"Killings? You mean that driver who was stabbed? Was there more than one?"

"Al Dwiri," she said. "You knew him."

"Real round shoulders, that guy? Walked sort of stooped over and read the racing form?"

"They cut his throat." Her eyes found mine and just as quickly darted away. They were brown with yellow flecks around the irises. I had never noticed before how pretty they were. "You would think that after maybe twenty years out there he wouldn't make mistakes," Frieda said. She paused. "Right. Okay. I hear they never took his money, he had over a hundred bucks on him. There was another guy around Christmas and in February too. Something's going on out there."

She had my full attention now. Her fright and her resolve were urgently communicating themselves to me while she did her best to appear cool.

"What do you hear?" I asked softly.

"Who knows? There's some kind of nutcase out there with a thing about taxi drivers. How do I know? The thing is, the drivers he's murdered, two of them anyhow, they knew enough not to take loads who look bad. I don't have to tell you, the wool watchcap pulled down over the eyebrows and the bulky coat. Him and his buddy, they jes' wanna go up the projects somewhere, they lookin' for Eu-gene's cousin. That's why it's so scary, Henry. You see? The killer must look like an ordinary shmo."

Her bag was in her lap. She opened it so I could see what was in it. Mace. "I never thought I needed it before," she said, and then let the straps fall. The soft bag folded closed again. "Right. The cops won't tell us anything except they're pursuing investigative leads. Very, very reassuring."

She shook a toothpick loose from the sugar shaker where Gino kept them and began picking at a particle of doughnut caught between two teeth.

"You have to be careful about dental hygiene," I said, remembering Seymour.

She looked puzzled. "What? I brush twice a day. That runt Lemon and his toadies down at Checker just smile when we ask any questions. And they're raising the gates to fifty bucks." Gates were the lease fee drivers paid. "We need to know more about what the hell is going on," Frieda said, and held aloft a particle of chocolate icing speared on her toothpick.

"Sounds like," I agreed.

"That's where you come in, darlin'. That's how come I'm risking my life drinking this coffee-flavored piss."

Gino laughed. He was standing at the register pretending not to be listening but in actual fact hanging on every word.

"Henry, how about giving the Alliance a hand?"

"I don't know, Frieda. I'm pretty busy right now."

"Right. I can get you money."

"You better," Gino said. "Otherwise how you going to support your beautiful daughters?"

Two

"I don't have all fucking day," Big John Lemon said as he came into the room where we were waiting upstairs at Checker Cab. "Let's hear it."

Before any of us had time to reply, the Checker Cab boss turned on Mel Dropo, his spear-carrier and general whipping boy. "Tell me when I gotta go," he ordered.

Mel glanced up at the large wall clock Big John could see too. Big John had plucked Mel out of a taxicab and made him an executive. The price of the job was the invisible welts across his back and the color of his nose. When he was sure his benefactor wasn't looking at him anymore, Dropo rolled his round brown eyes upward.

John Lemon wasn't any taller than five feet five. Everybody knew him as Big John, but nobody ever called him that to his face, which gave the irony a certain bite.

The other people in the room besides me were Frieda, another driver from the Alliance named John Geronimo, and the company's lawyer, Brian Scott. We were all seated in the Checker Cab conference room—a space cleared away in the middle of rows of gray metal filing cabinets where some schoolboy chairs were pulled up around an old light oak teacher's desk. Big John stayed on his feet. He crossed his arms over his thrusting chest and stared at Frieda, his mouth pulled into a disapproving line. "Well?"

"Right." She cleared her throat. "It's about the new medallions."

"I know that," he barked. You had to love this man.

"The Alliance is trying to make the mayor see sense," Frieda began again.

"Alliance!" It was an expletive.

"Are you denying our right to organize? Because the NLRB says that's not in question." John Geronimo's voice was shaking. He didn't know what to do with his hands, big worn mitts too large for his sinewy wrists and arms; he kept shifting them from his legs to the table and back, balling and unballing them. His pinched face was red with anger, anger and maybe a little bit of fright at the circumstances.

"Let's not get off on the wrong foot," suggested Brian Scott, the lawyer, in a deep booming voice. "Let's hear each other out, okay? I'm sure everybody in this room is in fundamental agreement that, to turn a phrase, taxi drivers are the unsung heroes of urban transportation, the city's unofficial goodwill ambassadors. We're here because of our common concerns about continued, uninterrupted first-class taxi service. So. Now. Tell us, if you will, Miss Mishkin. How can the company help?"

"The mayor's out to cut our throats," Frieda said. She giggled at her gruesome unintentional pun. "We need support."

"Support's our middle name." Mel Dropo kept a straight face.

Scott signaled concern by pursing his small, sensual lips. "The company, let me assure you, is against any rash and ill-timed restructuring of the industry. I think I'm on safe ground to venture the opinion, the personal opinion, that we all most certainly see eye to eye on that at least." You would have needed a Geological Survey map and a compass to find your way through the dense underbrush of equivocation in what Scott said, while managing to leave the impression of sympathy with Frieda.

"Come on, man, get off it!" This was Geronimo. "The company's in the mayor's hip pocket. You think we're idiots here?"

The blood rushed to Big John's face and the veins in his neck grew tense and prominent. The way he glared at Geronimo made me think he'd like to bite his head off. No metaphor intended.

Frieda said, "Nobody wants a strike, right? So what we need is to make her see sense before it gets too weird."

"Don't waste your breath," Geronimo told her. "I told you it was a waste of time."

"On the contrary," said Brian Scott, who stood up and put his hands on his hips. His suit coat was thrust back, revealing a roll of good living around his midriff. "Our good relations with the city government are necessary. Let's be realists— they exercise regulatory controls."

"What I think Brian is saying," I chimed in, "is that the company doesn't want the mayor to be unhappy. If she's unhappy, then the Bureau of Weights and Measures is unhappy. And if they're unhappy, the next time they certify the company gas pumps they might finally notice that little overcharge." It was only about 25 cents on a full tank, but when you're filling 250 captive tanks two shifts a day, 365 days a year the way Checker was, it added up to a lot of funny money.

Scott flushed. For all his pomposity, I liked what the flush showed about him.

"Our pumps are by the book! By the fucking book! You hear me?" It would have been hard not to, Big John was shouting. "What's Henry doing here? He doesn't drive for us anymore."

"He's consulting with the Alliance," Frieda said. "Aren't you, darlin'?" She threw me a nice warm grin, which I returned. I stretched my legs to ease the kinks. When you're six three and two hundred pounds, chairs built for schoolboys are an uncomfortable fit.

Big John shot me a withering look. What surprised me was that Geronimo did too.

"Are you people going to support us or what?" Frieda asked.

"I'm glad you see the good sense in seeking mutual objectives," Scott said.

But before he was able to continue, Mel Dropo asked, "How much?" Though the question was addressed to Frieda, he was looking at Big John,

"I don't know," she said. "Maybe a grand for the Alliance so we can get out the word about the protest at City Hall. And Ben's fee. That's all."

"Your money is not going to co-opt us," Geronimo said.

"C'mon, John, give them something to hope for," I said. Frieda roared.

"Henry?" Dropo asked.

"I get one hundred fifty a day."

"No fucking way. No. Fucking. Way." I thought Big John was agitated enough that he was about to start spinning and not stop 'til he reached Australia.

"John, " Brian Scott said. "This is something best discussed in private."

Without a word of goodbye Big John walked out, followed by Dropo. Before he went, too, Brian Scott said, "We'll be able to work something out. Good of you to come."

"Right. That's settled," Frieda said. She was grinning. "I told you your fee would be no problem."

"They're trying to co-opt us, that's all," Geronimo said.

"Of course they are, John," Frieda agreed.

"They want those new medallions just as much as Abigail. So long as the companies get them and not the independents."

"Right. John, look, we can't even afford to print a flier to alert the drivers about the demonstration at City Hall. Right now there's thirty-seven dollars in the cigar box. Second, darlin', we're going to hire ourselves a lawyer so when Scott and them start throwing legal curves at us, we have somebody to bat them back. That was Ben's idea. Their money gets us his help, and let's face it, you don't know how to get the dope on what these people are really up to, or to find out what the cops know about what's going on out there. He does.'' She pointed a thumb with a bright red nail at me.

"Oh, yeah?" He looked at the wall clock. "My cab's in."

When he had gone, Frieda said, "You know, sometimes I think we should drop all pretense of civilized behavior and get him and Big John alone in a room."

"They'd carry Geronimo out in little pieces."

"Right. I remember now, that's why I don't suggest it."

"Dropo's easier to deal with."

"Oh, Mel's much more reasonable, no question about it. Did you know his parents sued him for bilking them out of their home?"

Dropo's office door was open. He was behind his desk in a high-backed naugahyde swivel chair, looking out over the yard. There were 250 diagonal parking stalls in the yard, marked out in faded white paint, and a single semifunctional car wash. All but a few of the stalls were empty; the taxis were on the streets. I rapped once on the open door.

"What?" He didn't turn around.

On Dropo's desk were an empty set of wire baskets marked In and Out, a paper-clip dispenser in the shape of a golf ball, and a stack of manila files. A VDT sat on a typewriter table.

He swiveled to face me.

"Now what?"

"A taxi, Mel. Now and then."

"You're kidding, right?"

"The Alliance is hiring me to look into the drivers who were murdered."

"What drivers? What do you think you're talking about?"

"Albert Dwiri." I went into the inside pocket of my

chamois jacket and took out my pad. "Frank Iancini. Arnold Pachter. I talked with some people at the Hall. The M.O.'s the same on all of them, multiple stabs and a slit throat, but you already know that."

"That's a coincidence. These things always come in threes, like plane crashes."

"Thirty-nine years old," I read from my notes. "Two kids."

"He owned a pizzeria, too," Dropo said. "I used to eat there sometimes."

"It was Pachter who was thirty-nine and had the kids, not Iancini."

"Pachter, that's who I'm talking about. The Jew owned the pizzeria, that's San Francisco. Iancini didn't drive for us, he was with Metro. The cops are on top of that situation."

"They have people driving undercover?"

He shook his head. "Budgetary restraints."

"What kind of guy was this Pachter?"

Dropo stared at me forlornly: why was everybody busting *his* chops, his look said. He sighed. "A loudmouth. A lot of customer complaints." He waved a hand over the stack of files. "He drove like a fucking maniac. What difference does that make?"

"I don't know," I said, adopting a conversational tone, and crossing my legs. "Probably none. I'm just fishing, you know, for something that might."

"Dwiri, now, he was a heavy plunger." Dropo lowered his voice and glanced toward the open door. "Manchuco was left holding a lot of paper, that's what I hear."

"Manchuco? Why does that ring a bell?"

"His brother is Mercato, the one that runs for mayor, the nightclub guy who's going to bring the spirit of the samba to City Hall. He was a Republican too—can you believe that?"

"Republicans don't samba."

"No. Dwiri. A Republican taxi driver."

"And the Manchuco brother was his bookie?"

"Chris, yeah. He's got a back room in his real estate office out on Mission. Dwiri lived alone with his mother right around the corner on Godeus. This doesn't change anything. You can't drive a Checker unless you're bonded."

I waited.

"Shit." He slid an agreement toward me. Once I signed it I was bonded. But first I said, "Mel, how long you think it's going to be before Big John decides to recycle you back through the street?"

"You hear something?" He swiveled in his executive's chair so he was looking out over the yard.

I signed. "You have to stop making faces, Mel. He's got eyes in the back of his head, you know that."

Three

The fog had taken an evening off and the night was clear and soft, so I signed on as an extra, thinking that I had nothing else I had to do and there was no better time than right away to get back in touch with whatever was going on out there. The Life, as drivers—never call them cabbies, it has a George Bush ring to it—call their occupation. Prostitutes, another weary occupation, use the same phrase. The Life.

I made a precautionary pit stop in the Checker Cab lavatory where the new graffito was, "Management Never Sleeps," and just like that I was back on the street. No sooner was I out of the garage than I found myself immersed in a forgotten element, like a frog hopping from air to water and instinctively knowing how to breathe.

I let the tide of the night take me. My first ride was a flag downtown at Market and Sutter, a lady going to the Mid-Richmond, 21st Avenue. I decided on Turk instead of Pine heading west, and looked her over in the rearview mirror. Clerical or secretarial. Tired, end of a long day, takes a lot of cabs from work—maybe there's a latchkey kid at home.

"Great to be going home, huh?" I met her black eyes and smiled.

"Boy, you said it. The kids keep me busier than my boss, but I can't wear slippers at Tepper, Klondike, Potter and Wright."

We laughed; then she sighed, leaned back, drifted. The only other time we talked was when I was sailing along Turk up near Lincoln University and she said, "The lights are timed a little better." A great way to begin, a ride as comfortable as a forty-year marriage. The tip, of course, was exactly right.

It's a generalization, but people who think of themselves as working people—whatever that means in an age of information—are usually good tippers. If they're high, or in an especially good mood, or in love, or have just won a lot of money at poker or bingo or the stock market, then they tip generously. Also, some very pretty women, women who enjoy being memorable, sometimes make a point of being lavish tippers. Younger professional women, yupsters, pretty or not, are tight-fisted, I think because they want to show they're nobody's fool. Other women use their sex appeal to hustle drivers. The very first night I ever drove a taxi I had a girl who leaned her elbows on top of the front seat and talked with me from just beside my right ear as if I were a pretty special guy. So this is what taxi-driving is all about, I thought as I ran Cybil, because that was her name, on errands from Seacliff to south of Market. The meter was thumping away in time with my heart. Cybil had me wait for her while she dashed into her Russian Hill apartment to change her clothes, she said, and get some more money. After she was inside for a while I began to notice how big the building was and how many apartments there were in it. After about fifteen minutes I came to grips with the fact that Cybil had disappeared from my life forever.

It was miraculous how the moment I had slipped behind the wheel again, turned on the motor, and listened to the rumbling whine that only taxicabs make, that throbbing impatience, this river of old knowledge came running swiftly back from wherever it had dried up when I wasn't in The Life. In London, England, they called what a taxi driver had to know The Knowledge. It took years of study, you had to master every crooked turn in that beehive city, before you were licensed to drive one of those classy black mariahs. In San Francisco if you had the license fee and no criminal record, they sent you out on your own. Now here I was behind the wheel again, hoping to come across somebody bad who might be passing for sad.

What could I hope to accomplish pretending, or maybe not pretending, to be a cab driver again? The best I could hope for was the worst I could hope for, that some psychopath would try to turn me into food for worms. Caught up in these thoughts, I had been in a fugue state. I snapped back to find that I was near Holly Park Circle, where the driver Albert Dwiri had been killed. I could feel his fright as he was being stabbed. I sped away from there, down the hill toward the lighted storefronts and peopled sidewalks of Mission Street, and realized that I was only a few blocks south of Chris Manchuco's real estate office.

As I drove by I saw somebody inside working late—it was well past dark—and I pulled into a bus zone and stopped. What the hell, why not? I got out and tapped on the glass door. The man inside came and unbolted two locks, threw the chain, and told me, "I didn't call for a cab."

He looked from me to the taxi and back again. The face wore a smile but was watchful. His suit was shiny and expensive, his satiny shirt was open three buttons showing off a taut, hairless chest and a triple gold chain, and his aviator glasses were yellow-tinted. He looked like a refugee from *Miami Vice*.

"That's okay," I said. "I'm not a cab driver."

"That's your taxi."

"So? This is your real estate office, but there's more going on than just real estate, right, Mr. Manchuco?"

His hand came off the door knob in a way that conveyed readiness and suspicion.

"My name is Ben Henry," I said. "I'm making some inquiries about the murder of Albert Dwiri. I'd appreciate it if you would give me a few minutes."

"You a reporter?"

I shook my head.

"You ain't out of Mission station. I know all the boys from over there."

"That's a good thing in these times; it must make you sleep better at night. No, I'm private."

"What's it to me?" He was wary but no longer so tense. Reporters, cops, thieves—they all represented different kinds of problems. Private he could handle.

"A few minutes?"

"Okay, my friend, you want to talk, Chris Manchuco will try and be a help." He stepped back and when I was inside he closed the door behind me and relatched the chain. There was a ledger book open on his desktop which he reached over and shut before sliding it into a desk drawer. The room was lit by two tracks of bright fluorescent tubes. One segment flickered as if it had a case of bad nerves. Manchuco gestured me into a chair beside his desk, but instead of sitting himself, he walked over to a closed door at the back of the one large room and opened it a crack.

"Jorge," he called, and said something in Spanish, looking at me the whole time. Then he shut the door again. When he had settled into his own chair he said to me, "A terrible thing about poor Albert, they say his throat was cut. Right here in our own neighborhood. You are not from San Francisco, are you, Mr. . . . ?"

"Henry, Ben Henry. No, not originally."

"Then you only know what is here now, you can't know how our neighborhood has changed. The entire city, yes, but the Mission the most of all. Take it from Chris Manchuco, things have gone down and now they will begin up again. You know how long the Manchucos are in the Mission? Thirty-five years, no, more, my father came in the War. Okay, tell me, what do you think I know to tell you about what happened to Albert?"

"They say he owed you money when he died."

"Who is it that has hired a suave investigator like your-self?" He pronounced it "swah-vey."

I needed a shave and I was dressed in scuffed old boots with worn-out heels, faded Levi's, a Giants sweatshirt, and a windbreaker. I was dressed for driving, not question-asking.

"I'm working for the Taxicab Alliance. Did he?"

He stared as if I had not spoken. The silence became a challenge. This guy in shiny pants with no belt loops was throwing down the gauntlet. I sighed and stood up.

"I'll go ask Jorge, then," I said, and went for the door to the back room. I opened the door. There was no light but I could make out a chalkboard already filled in with the next day's daily double entries and the morning line for Bay Meadows and Santa Anita. Lots of telephones and standing ashtrays, but no Jorge.

"You think careful about it, Mr. Henry," Manchuco said from behind me. "What do I want to see poor Albert dead for? Do you think Chris Manchuco is ever going to see the money that is his from the hand of a dead man? Now you get out of my place. *Pronto!*"

"Jorge must have popped out for a taco or something," I said, and started for the front door.

"Hey, Mr. Henry. Mr. Ben Henry." I turned and we faced each other across the room. "You got a friend out here in the Mission, you remember that. Chris Manchuco and his broth-ers, we watch out for you anytime you come out our way."

Four

From where I was waiting at the top of the steps leading to the Hall of Flowers in Golden Gate Park, I spotted Jessica Gage coming toward me along the path as soon as she appeared beyond the hedge. I had arrived early because it wouldn't do to keep her waiting alone in the park, or anywhere else.

She wore a black cotton shift, cinched at the waist with a wide yellow belt. The neckline was scooped out, and around her long neck was a single strand of round milky-yellow stones. The skirt, which ended an inch or two above her knees, had a lot of swish when she moved in it. So did her straight, shoulder-length black hair. It was gleaming black, very uncharacteristic for an English girl, she had told me. Jessica looked as cool as the other side of the pillow.

She waved as she came closer, and we both started to laugh. She threw herself into my arms.

"While I was coming up the steps and you were coming down, were you thinking of a television commercial?"

"For a shampoo," I said. "Slo-mo, running through a field of wildflowers."

"It did seem like that. Did you have good news? It's nice here, isn't it? I've never been inside this conservatory, have you? Why are we meeting here? Well, tell me your news, out with it, laddie."

"Wait a minute. How do you know I have any news?"

"You should see yourself. You're all puffed up and you're wearing your macho-man jeans and you're barely able to listen to a word I'm saying because you're just waiting your chance to tell me whatever it is. I expect it's a new client, isn't it? Some case you've got. It's better than the runaway you found at Krishna House, though, isn't it? I can see it is."

"I don't understand how you could know all that."

Jessica rested her hip against mine. "You do perfectly well understand. Let's walk." We started down the steps. "You're about as difficult to read as a yield sign. Have you ever wondered about those signs? I mean, who else but the Americans would post signs that said yield? Supine, I obey. Well?"

"We're meeting here," I said, "because I wanted to see you against the lush green of the park, first of all. As for the Hall of Flowers, it has some qualities I liked as a backdrop for you. A kind of wedding-cake frivolity. And something that conjures up words like 'taj' and 'casbah.' "

"Harem."

"Harem." I laughed and dropped my hand over her hip, feeling it roll beneath my fingers as we walked. Her long, sinuous arms were bare and she wore three bracelets on her slim left wrist. One was jade, which matched the color of her knowing eyes.

"This is all very bright for you. Compared, say, to the cemetery tour of Colma."

"Our second date. When I told you about Pretty Boy Floyd."

"What exactly did the Pretty Boy say when the sheriff gunned him down?"

"Ranger, it was a ranger named Noonan. After Noonan shot him in the back—he'd been trailing Pretty Boy for years but never caught up because people who hated bankers as much as Pretty Boy, it was the Depression, hid him—Noonan walked over and stood over him. 'Well, Pretty Boy, I guess you have a lot of friends.' Pretty Boy was dying. He held out his hand. 'My name is Charles Arthur Floyd. Will you be my friend?' "

"Your hands are never still," she said.

"Not around you, no."

She twisted away from my hand and laughed. "Or your mind, or your mouth, or your hair. You have kinetic hair."

We linked arms and kept walking.

"Well, are you going to tell me, then?"

"When have I had a chance with the way you babble?"

"And whose fault is that? Go ahead, hurry up, out with it, Hank, I'm dying to hear your news."

"Hank?"

"It's American. Short for Henry."

"The trouble with women today is they don't know their place," I said.

"Ah, but I do know my sign."

"Your sign? Oh, Christ, Jessica, have the pod people gotten you too?" I stopped walking.

She looked me right in the eye, smiling without moving her lips. "Yield."

"Ah." We walked a few steps in silence, a silence dense with inchoate language. "I forget," I said. "Have I mentioned that I've taken on a new case?"

"I don't believe you did, actually. Anything interesting?"

"Not really. A murder. Three murders, in fact. And the culprit still at large. I don't think there's anything there for a novelist's sensibilities."

"Well, yes, it is a bit tame for the Sussex taste."

"I knew it would be. They were cab drivers."

"We do have a taxi in Stelling, you know. And suicides, but not any murders. Not that we know of, that is. How did they die?"

"Their throats were slit."

"Oh, that's ghastly," she said.

"I know. The cops and the companies aren't telling the

drivers what they know, if they know anything. The situation is a little complicated. The drivers are trying to organize a union in what's been a feudal industry. Feudalism with V-8 motors. The means of production are owned by the company and they lease the cabs to the drivers. When it pleases the company they levy fines. If a driver lets out a peep of protest about his working conditions or anything else, he's gone. There's a million other guys out there with as much brains in their right foot waiting to take his place. It's a lousy, unhealthy life, but how many other jobs requiring virtually no skills put a hundred or a hundred fifty in cash in your pocket, off the books, at the end of every shift?

"The mayor figures in it, too—she wants to put a lot more taxis on the street for the Democratic convention, taxis that will still be there when the delegates go home. It means a big loss of income for the drivers. So the combination of the economic screwing and the fact that somebody's slicing them up and nobody from the cops to City Hall will tell them the way to San Jose, well, the drivers are so scared and angry anything could happen.

"Anyway, the gal who is organizing the drivers is named Frieda Mishkin. She drives for Checker, the industry giant. She's got the company to pay my fee. They're hoping to keep the drivers quiet; Frieda's hoping I'll help stop them from screwing the drivers again."

"And the killer? What do you know about him?"

"Very little so far. He stabs drivers until they're disabled and then he cuts them a second mouth just below the jawline. One of the drivers was a horseplayer and he owed a lot of money to a bookie."

"Bookmakers are illegal here, aren't they? Your puritanism shows in the most surprising ways. I mean, the whole country springs from this restless, gambling spirit, and then you make wagering illegal. This is why everybody in the world is so wary of America, you see—it's so unpredictable in its moralism. So the bookie is a kind of criminal?"

"Well, a lowlife idiot is closer to it. But he and I have talked and understand each other."

"What will you do next?"

"I've got a couple of ideas. And I went out and drove for a while last night."

"You're driving a taxi again?" She looked away.

"No, not really. Undercover, if that doesn't sound too melodramatic."

"You want to be careful."

"Don't worry, I'll be fine," I said breezily. Then I looked at her face. "I will be," I said.

"Never mind I won't be here."

My heart sank—she was returning home to England. "Where are you going to be?" I tried to keep what I was feeling out of my face and my voice.

"I'm going home for a while. But what is this Frieda person like, then?"

"Frieda? I don't know, she's okay. Very gutsy, thoroughly frightened by the whole situation, very determined, funny. I like her. She's been driving a while but her first love is opera. She sings contralto in semi-professional productions. When?"

"Monday. She's very beautiful, I suppose?"

"Monday. Why didn't you tell me sooner?"

"I didn't suppose it would matter very much to you."

"What does that mean?"

"Well, you've got your Frieda to keep you company, don't you?"

"Frieda? Why are you going? How long for?"

"Is there any reason I shouldn't be?"

"I didn't mean it that way," I said. "Oh, Christ."

"What did you mean, then?"

Suddenly we were in each other's arms, holding on tightly. It was the first time we had ever hugged like that, as reassurance rather than romance. We held each other for what seemed like a long, long time. Finally Jessica stepped back.

Her lips looked warm and swollen and especially dark and soft. She half turned away.

Beyond her in a meadow an after-work softball game was in progress, the ball players on each side wearing matching caps and jerseys, but all different pants and shoes. There were two runners on base.

"The university has asked me to stay on for another year and I've agreed. I hope you're not displeased. I'm going home to arrange for some of my things to be shipped here. And I have business in London with my agent and my publisher. There are friends I miss whom I haven't had a good gossip with in ages."

"Displeased? Oh, Christ, Jessica, I'm delighted. I know what you told me is all true, but it's not the whole truth."

"Michael deserves an explanation of why I'm staying," she said.

"Yes, he does," I agreed. It was good to pay particular attention to how a woman leaves the man she leaves for you. Who knows when your turn will come?

The batter tagged one and sent a rocket into the chest of a surprised shortstop, who threw up his glove in self-defense. His momentum sent him stumbling toward second, where he easily doubled off the runner. His teammates were screaming, "First! First!" His throw beat the second runner to the bag, completing the triple play.

"Damn! Did you see that?"

"See what?"

"A triple play. I've never seen one of those before." I could see her puzzlement. "The baseball game." I pointed. "Everything is going to be fine, Jessica. I'll be right here waiting when you get back."

She didn't even glance at the game in the meadow but looked right into my face.

"I think we had better go to your place, Hank," she said. Then she dropped her eyes shyly.

Five

The glass doors of the international terminal hissed open ahead of her. She didn't look back as I watched her hastily fall in with the crowds of travelers. The doors closed.

She was gone and something had gone with her. An aura. Jessica Gage took me right out of myself at the same time she brought me right home. Being with her had a clarity and a rhythm known only to us.

I drove slowly back up the middle lane of the Bayshore toward the city. I double-checked to be sure my headlights were on after several drivers passing me in the fast lane stared at me curiously. I think it was just that I was in a cab—I had thought that taking her to her flight in a taxi might amuse her—and going slow. How often do you see a slow taxi?

For all that our conversations seemed never to cease, not even when we were apart, I didn't have much I wanted to say about Jessica. Not to anybody else, not to myself.

The dispatch radio was playing softly, the murmur of intersections a kind of night music; but now I heard something in the tone of what Doris was saying that made me turn the radio up louder.

"Checker 598, over; Checker 598, over." There was no response on the monitor. "Drivers, we have an all points bulletin on cab 598. Anyone seeing 598, give us his location, please. Repeat, anyone seeing 598, give us his location. Do not—do not—approach the cab yourself."

I picked up my hand mike and checked in.

"Is that the former 626?" Doris said. "Welcome back, worse luck."

On the monitor a driver with a heavy Eastern European accent said, "Hello, this is 626. I am down here by the Fisherman's Wharf. You call for me, please?"

"Forget it, driver," Doris said. "I was talking to somebody else."

"Where's the last you heard from 598?" I asked her.

"About two hours ago he dropped Esther at the Stop-A-While. I gave him another pickup but he never showed." Esther was a regular rider, a widow who went from her home to the tavern every night, and then back home again at closing time. For some obscure reason she was the only person in San Francisco whose personal checks were accepted by the company, a single article of faith in a dense codicil of commerce.

"I'm out that way," I told Doris. "I'll cruise around, maybe I'll find 598. He's probably tucked in with Esther."

"Check," she said. "Let me know."

Esther was plastered to a bar stool in the Stop-A-While, but there was no sign of 598. I nosed down Mission Street and then took Persia up the hill into McLaren Park, which was dark and foreboding. The park was a wild place, a rendezvous for assignations, gang fights, junkies cooking up. From time to time a body showed up there, usually somebody from the beat and broken housing projects at the east end of the park. At Silliman I doubled back and started west again, running now through a neighborhood of working-class bungalows with barred windows and gates. It was silly, really: Checker 598 could be anywhere in the city, forty-six square miles.

As I crossed University a light at the periphery of my vision caught my attention, way up by the reservoir. Was that a taxi with its dome light lit? At that distance I wasn't sure. As I drew closer I saw that it was a cab with both streetside doors agape. I came up slowly. Checker 598. Nobody was visible inside. To my left was the concrete expanse of the old reservoir, a long, flat, empty space. To my right was the edge of McLaren Park. It was as deserted a place as you were likely to find inside the city limits.

I got out cautiously, straining to see into the shadows. My heart was thumping. I approached the abandoned cab. The motor wasn't running but the radio was broadcasting: I could hear Doris calling intersections. With my senses straining against the dark, and the unnerving isolation, I slowly came up to the open doors. The driver was crumpled beneath the steering wheel over the pedals, in an attitude too awkward for life. His hand, covered in blood, was lifted and the fingers were bent, as if he had been clawing at something. There were long bloody cuts along the insides of his fingers.

I leaned in, feeling vulnerable along the length of my exposed spine. There was a heavy odor of burning, and of cigar, in the cab. The seat was soaked in blood that had begun to thicken and turn black. What I saw brought a heave of nausea up from my stomach, carrying an ugly metallic taste into my throat. His head hung beside his shoulder, attached to his neck by a few strands of bloody sinew and muscle. I choked back my fright and my sickness. A noise behind me made me whirl, my hands in front of me to ward off an attack. Nobody was there.

I took a deep breath before leaning back into the cab. This time I saw the source of the burning smell; there was a half-smoked, extinguished cigar that had burned a hole in his pants before it went out. I opened the lid of a cigar box on the front seat. Besides his smokes, it contained coins and neatly piled bills, a loose stack of singles and then a folded bunch of larger bills with a rubber band around it. Clipped to the visor was the waybill, filled out in pencil. The driver's name, written in at the top, was Greg White. The last entry was a pickup at San Jose and Onandaga, not far from the Stop-A-While. No destination.

Then I saw it, scrawled on the windshield in what looked like grease pencil, three characters from some other alphabet. I recognized them as Hebrew, a language I had hardly seen since I dropped my bar mitzvah lessons after my father died. I wasn't certain, but I thought the characters were Aleph Mem Tof. They meant something, I couldn't remember what. As I studied them a rivulet of what looked like blood ran out of the Mem and trickled across the windshield, making my knees weak. The grease pencil must have been dipped in blood. I backed out of the cab, retching, and looked swiftly all around me again.

I looked carefully into the back floor of my own cab before I got in. Doris was just giving a driver an address. I waited until she was finished and then checked in with a code blue. She didn't hear me at first and I had to repeat it.

"Clear the air, drivers, I've got a code blue." On the monitor I could hear several drivers calling their locations, bidding on calls. "Wait a sec, drivers, hold your horses. I've got a code blue, I said, clear the air. Go ahead, 523, where are you?"

"Up by the reservoir at University and, oh, hell, I don't know, Dwight? Woolsey? I found 598."

"You need the code blues, Ben? I'm getting them on the phone right now. What's the matter?"

"He's dead."

"Say what?"

"Dead, the driver, Greg White. He's been stabbed, he's dead."

"Oh, jeez louise. Hold on, I've got the police on the line. Are you all right?"

"I'm fine."

"You better get out of there. Hold it. All right, the police are on the way. Drive down to Silver and University; they'll meet you there.''

I could hear a chorus of anxious drivers asking what was wrong. I switched them off and went to the police band on the monitor. Doris said, ''Shut up! Everybody shut up! Five-two-three, over.''

''I'm listening. What?''

''You getting out of there?''

''It doesn't matter. I'll wait here.''

''Check. You be careful. Jeez louise.''

The police dispatcher called the possible 187, the statute number for a homicide, and gave the location. I lit a cigarette to get the taste of regurgitated fright out of my mouth. In just a moment I heard a police siren bleating like a cow being slaughtered, and then a police cruiser was tearing up the street toward me, its lights pulsating. I got out of my cab to meet them.

Both cops emerged with their guns drawn. They had the high-intensity beam shining in my eyes, partially blinding me.

''Put your hands up where we can see them,'' one of the cops shouted. He stayed behind the shield of the open door of the prowl car, his pistol leveled at me.

I did exactly as he said. ''A driver's been killed,'' I said. ''He's in the other cab, 598. I found him.''

Both cops advanced toward me. One stopped with his service revolver trained on my midriff. The other went past and looked into 598. He returned to the prowl car and got on his radio. The cop who was watching me said, ''I want your driver's license and then I want you against the hood with your legs spread and your hands behind the fucking head.''

He was young. A short, slim Chinese, bareheaded. He seemed as nervous as I was. I did as he told me. He handed my license in to his partner, who got on his radio again and ran a check on me while the Chinese kid patted me down. Two more police cars, their sirens keening, wheeled into the street one after the other. Lights began to go on in houses far down the block. Somebody opened a front door and came out into the street to watch.

"What are you doing here?" the young cop asked me.

"We had an all points bulletin on 598, he had gone missing. I was looking for him."

"Oh, yeah? How come?"

"I just told you."

He moved toward me threateningly. "You going to give me lip, huh?"

His partner said, "Take it easy, Wayne. Sergeant's on his way. And Homicide."

A fourth prowl car arrived. You could hear all their radios broadcasting simultaneously through the open windows. There was a lot of activity, and nothing happening. I threw my cigarette down and lit another. In a few minutes I heard an ambulance siren, a different kind of yelping wail from the police sirens. The cops were setting up a line to keep back the crowd that was gathering. A new black Buick slid up and was waved through the line. I knew the detective who got out of the Buick. His name was Browder. His face was still partially swollen with sleep.

"Who's the investigating officer?" he asked the uniform closest to him.

"Over there," the cop said, nodding in the direction of the kid who was still keeping a close eye on me. "Hsu."

Browder had flat feet and walked over to the boy named Hsu looking down at the ground with his hands in his jacket pockets. He was an old hand who had been in Homicide for years. Squat, with a furrowed brow, deep-set eyes, a little mustache, and a hairline receding on either side of a widow's peak.

"What's Henry doing here?" he asked Officer Hsu.

"He reported the 187, sir. Says he happened to be looking for the missing taxi. That other one's his taxi."

"Well?" Browder said to me.

"I'm working for the drivers' Alliance, Jimmy," I told Browder. "This guy was stabbed, too—his head's severed. No money taken."

"I guess I can go home and fall asleep in front of the television again," Browder said. "You already did my job for me. C'mon, tell me what happened." He began to walk toward 598. I went with him, explaining how I came to be there and what I had found. He seemed hardly to be listening, but I knew he was taking it all in and, like all cops, suspecting the truth of everything he was hearing.

A television reporter approached us. I didn't know his name, but his face was familiar. Perfect cheekbones, expensive barber. "What have we got here, Inspector?" The voice—oh, the voice.

"What the fuck?" Browder said. "Get this guy behind the line. Get him away from the scene," he shouted. Two uniforms came rushing forward.

"I need my camera in here," the TV guy said. "We may be going live at eleven. We're the Action News remote team. Channel Six."

"Sure, I know you, George, sure," Browder said. "But listen, you have to go over there behind the line until I get a chance to do my job here. We'll let you in later. How ya doin'?"

"We're live in twenty minutes, Inspector. We'll want to do a feed with you." He looked at his Rolex.

"Yeah, sure."

"Are you the one who found the body?" He was talking to me. "Did you witness the crime?" He waved his cameraman toward us. "Hurry up, for crissake."

"I told you, George, you and your camera guy behind the line."

"Just step over here with us," Action George said to me. "Are you a cabbie? That's your cab over there, right? Get him against the taxi," he told his cameraman. "What's your name, sir?"

"You want to talk to him?" Browder asked me.

"Talk to who?"

We turned and went toward 598. Action George yelled after us, "George Wilson, Action News Team. Sir. Just a word. Your name? Do you know the dead cabbie? How did it happen?"

Browder and I walked a few steps in silence. "What a fucking racket," he said.

I didn't know if he meant his, or Action George's, and I didn't ask.

There was a sergeant waiting at the open door of 598. Greg White's blood-soaked corpse, its head dangling, was still where I had found it.

"How you doin', Walter?"

"Pretty good, Jimmy. Can't complain. How's your dad?"

"Got his handicap down to fourteen," Browder told the sergeant.

"Tell him I asked."

"He'll be glad to hear. You seen Corelli?" Corelli was Browder's partner.

The sergeant shook his head. Browder sighed before he leaned into the cab and took a slow, careful look around without touching anything. He took a handkerchief out and opened the lid of the cigar box and then closed it again. The sergeant shone his flashlight at the windscreen, illuminating the Aleph Mem Tof with the trickle of dried blood curling away from the Mem.

"Okay," Browder said.

"You find the same writing with Dwiri?" I asked him when he had backed out of the cab.

"Yes." He didn't show any surprise that I knew about that.

"And the other ones? Iancini? Pachter?"

"Not the first one These last three. Any weapon?" he asked the sergeant.

"No, not yet, Jimmy. I got men looking around the reservoir and the park, but we'll be able to do more in the morning. A sharp blade, that's the way it looks."

Browder went to the crime lab boys, who were standing nearby holding their metal cases, and told them what he wanted. His hands were deep in his pockets when he returned to me.

"They going to find your prints in there?"

I nodded.

"Great," he said.

"You have any idea what it's about?" The police photographer was shooting inside the cab, his flash popping.

He shook his head. "Not really."

"What does the Hebrew mean? I used to know." I remembered a classroom in the synagogue on the south side of Chicago, not far from the university. The memory came complete with the ennui of being indoors on a warm spring day, the dust motes turning in a beam of rose-colored light where the sunshine passed through the tinted glass window. The letters were chalked on a portable blackboard with a green writing surface. I could remember all that useless detail, but not what the rabbi had been saying.

"Truth," Browder told me. "It's the new ecumenical spirit—the chief got a rabbi who consults for us. The chaplain's still one of our own, thank God. Aleph Mem Tof—truth." The Aleph sounded like "olive" in Browder's mouth.

"The Lord moves in mysterious ways," I said.

"So do I. Where the fuck is that Corelli?"

"You going to talk to Action News?"

"Got to."

"What are you going to tell them?"

"I don't want the whole town's nuts in an uproar. Look, I got a lot to do here. You come by tomorrow morning, give us a statement."

"Browder! Browder!" Somebody with a foghorn for a voice was yelling. I looked in the direction of the voice. It was a short, corpulent man, as agitated as he was wide, being restrained behind the police line by a uniform. He wore a cab driver's badge attached to a cap from the National Rifle Association. "It was a jig, right, Browder? One of the brothers?"

"They're crawling out of the toilet bowls. You know him? Bryant, Joe Bryant. They call him the Fat Man?"

"No. You think he knows the dead driver was black?"

"It wouldn't matter to him. He needs killing himself. He's a badge sniffer, always hanging around Homicide. I'll see you in the morning."

I walked back toward my cab. An airplane passed high overhead with a long, aspirated whisper. Jessica was somewhere out over the continent. I felt a stab of apprehension. As I reached my cab, I saw a man sitting in the front seat on the passenger side.

"Nellie Flynn," I said in surprise when I was close enough to recognize him.

"*The Courier*, cabbie, step on it." Nellie was the police reporter for the morning newspaper. Once upon a time we had worked together. His slitted, red-rimmed eyes looked me over shrewdly.

"It's going to cost you a drink. I've got a bad taste in my mouth and a serious case of nerves."

"Let's go. Home edition closes in half an hour."

I moved the taxi slowly forward until I found enough space to make a U-turn. The crime lab boys were working in 598 now, and the coroner's team was standing by with a gurney. A cop moved a sawhorse to let me by. I was edging through the people and the vehicles when I saw Action George waiting for me. I didn't stop, so he began to jog beside my open window, trailed by his technician. He had a microphone pointed toward my face. The high intensity light from the Betacam was shining in my eyes.

"Just a word, sir. Will you speak to Action News?"

"No problem," I said, and kept rolling. There was one sure way of keeping myself out of his report, and I retained the old newsman's aversion to appearing before the camera. "Heavy fucking traffic for this time of night, George. A real fucking bitch." I smiled at him.

"Visuals," Nellie said. "Don't forget the visuals." He lifted a middle finger toward the camera.

"Nothing fucking personal, George." The road ahead of me was clear. I accelerated.

"Whoa," Nellie said. "He forgot to ask you how you felt finding that poor slob's body."

"Wretched. Frightened. You can quote me."

"I could quote you in *The Courier* as easily as I could"— he looked down at the spiral pad in his knobbly hand—"Greg White." There had been some differences of opinion between *The Courier* and me in the past.

"There's always our old friend, a source close to the investigation."

"Sergeant back there said you found the body, he didn't mention you were doing an investigation."

When I didn't respond, Nellie said, "Oh, you want me to ask you questions. Like a reporter."

I had to laugh. "What else did the sergeant say?"

"Head severed," Nellie began, flipping back through his notes. "Apparently a sharp blade, not found. No apparent theft. And some funny writing on the front window."

"Hebrew."

"No, he's in my parish, St. Cecilia's, Sergeant Walter V for Vincent O'Malley."

"The Writing, it's Hebrew. There's more. This is the fourth cab driver to get sliced up like this since December. Two of the other three had the same letters found in their cabs. You think you can make a story out of that?"

"Light feature, maybe."

I thought it was a good idea to go public. Couldn't hurt in the department of sympathy for cab drivers, and if the Alliance was bucking the mayor, they'd need public sympathy. And every driver in the city would be warned.

"What are the letters?" Nellie said.

"Don't use this, okay? Browder may need it to sort out somebody legitimate from the lunatic hordes. But they're Aleph Mem Tof. It means truth."

"Very Old Testament." He snapped his fingers. "Got it! The Prophet of Doom."

"Never. Not even *The Courier*. No chance, pal."

Six

The headline pushed at the edges of *The Courier*'s front page: FOURTH CABBIE HACKED TO DEATH/BY "PROPHET OF DOOM" KILLER. I carried the paper upstairs, reading as I went. True to his word, Nellie had omitted Aleph Mem Tof from his story, and had written only that an ancient language had provided the police with an important clue. A manhunt was under way, Nellie's story said, for a killer—and this was the word I loved—*dubbed* the "Prophet of Doom." Who done the dubbing he did not say. But just so we wouldn't miss the point, he invoked the sobriquets of weirdos past from Army, Symbionese Liberation, through Zebras and Zodiac.

"Oh, Be-en," Peter said when I dialed the service, "it is a glorious day today. We are so truly fortunate to be alive."

"Beats being dead, Peter. Now, if we were only rich, eh?"

"Money is shit, Be-en."

"But God did invent toilet paper, Peter."

"It is just a pose, your negativity, Be-en. You would do better to look inside you for what embraces the positive. I am still of course practicing my Hatha yoga, but since I have come to the path of Swami Muktananda, the way is peaceful. It is up to each of us to create peace, Be-en. I think you are a borderline type A, but please do not take offense at my personal observation."

Which came first, California or the seekers? I lit the day's first cigarette.

"You are sad today, Be-en?"

No, I just want my messages. I didn't say it, though. What I said was, "Just taking a cleansing breath, Peter. Tell me, no rush or anything but I would like to know, any messages for me?"

"Well, yes, Be-en. I was just looking to see if any of them would be uplifting of your spirits. So let me see, yes, a Miss Frieda called. I did not get the last name. She wants to remind you to meet her at her home at eleven o'clock; she is in need of a lift to the demonstration. And a Mr. Dropo called, too. He said he must speak to you about an incident. He is an abrasive man, this Mr. Dropo."

"I couldn't agree more."

"I tried to talk with him about this, but he hung up the phone."

"No! Really? Any other messages?"

"That is the lot of them. How is our Jessica? I have not heard from her in a beaver's age."

I glanced at the time and added eight hours. She had landed in London while I was still asleep. I imagined her husband meeting her plane, an embrace. Dammit. "She's gone home to England for a visit." I dragged on the cigarette.

"She will be back when?"

I tried to look for what embraced the positive. "Soon, Peter. Well, I'll catch you later."

"Yes, Be-en. And, Be-en, you really cannot make a proper cleansing breath with a cigarette in your mouth, you know."

I decided to put off seeing Browder until after the demonstration at City Hall, and instead pored over the box scores in the paper until it was time to meet Frieda at her place in the Haight. She came to the door not in her usual denims but in a light wool skirt and sweater. She had applied lipstick and eye shadow, and when she pecked at my cheek I caught a whiff of her perfume.

"We are smart today," I said. I was wearing a poplin suit and a maroon knit tie.

"Got to look my best for my public, darlin'. Come on in, I was hoping you'd notice."

I couldn't think of a reply to the coquetry, and there was a brief, stilted silence. Frieda's place was a San Francisco Victorian flat, laid out like a boxcar along a narrow hallway. The kitchen at the rear and the front sitting room were bright with sunlight, but the passageway and the bedrooms were dim. A black-and-white mongrel dog came trotting up to me, its nails tapping on the hardwood floor, and began to mount my ankle.

"Get down, Malcolm," Frieda said.

I scratched behind its ears.

"He's never learned any manners," Frieda said indulgently. She led the way into the front room. The furniture—an overstuffed wing chair, a sofa, bookcases, an inexpensive stereo, two standing lamps with tassels hanging from the shades, and a pair of Mexican cowhide chairs—was worn but not disreputable. She kept the place both neat and clean.

I chose one of the Mexican chairs, and Frieda sank onto the sofa. "Nothing like another dead driver to whet the appetite of the media for the issues," she said. "They're all coming to the demo. That was you who found Greg White last night, wasn't it? In 523?"

I nodded.

"Horrible?" She wrinkled up her pug nose.

"Horrible. Did you know about what the paper called writing from an ancient language?"

She shook her head. "No. Tell me, darlin'." The last word came out breathless. She was scared, so I told her as completely and as ungraphically as I could.

When I finished she didn't move or speak for an instant

before she said, "Okay. Right. Well, it's awful to say so, but I suppose this Prophet of Doom—where do they dig these names up from anyway?—can't be all bad for the Alliance, can he?"

"Yeah, I had the same thought. Did you know Greg White?"

"A little. He always had a cigar stuck in his mouth, it smelled godawful."

"Frieda, can you think of anything to connect him to the other drivers who were killed? Anything they might all have had in common?"

"Besides that they were drivers, you mean? No, not really. The only one I really knew well was Arnold."

"Did he smoke cigars?"

"You think the Prophet of Doom's an antismoking zealot, darlin'? No, the only thing Arnold smoked was dope. Listen, I got a pot of fresh coffee out in the kitchen. And a chocolate cake."

"Just the coffee, thanks."

"You take milk and sugar?"

"Yeah."

"We're organizing a collection for his family, Greg's. Here, look this over." It was a Xerox copy of an appeal I assumed was going to be posted at the different taxi yards. Frieda left the room, followed by Malcolm. I put aside the appeal and went over to the painted white shelves built into alcoves on either side of a fireplace with a marble mantelpiece. The shelves closer to the bay windows that overlooked the Panhandle were crammed with mementos and artifacts. There were opera programs from productions in which Frieda had performed; a collection of lapel buttons from demonstrations and causes past; a soft tweed cap with a taxicab pin on the beak; pieces of driftwood, sea-smoothed colored glass, and seashells including a conch; and some miniature china dolls. Among the photographs was one that came as a surprise. I was still looking at it when Frieda came back into the room, carrying our coffee mugs in one hand and a wedge of chocolate cake in the other. With her in a soft skirt and sweater, I noticed the way she moved before her size. Her pillowy body was a place of comfort.

She placed the mugs and her plate on a low table in front of the couch, sat down again, and forked a slice of cake into her mouth.

"This is you, right?" I was holding the photograph.

"Maybe. I'm not trying to sound mysterious, darlin'. It's sure as hell what I looked like circa 1973." She laughed. "I put on a little bit of weight since then."

The girl in the photograph was shapely, with the long straight hair that had been the style of the day on the un-adorned Left.

Frieda was watching me closely. "You like that," she said.

I put the photograph back in its place and went to the Mexican chair, ignoring her position in the middle of the sofa, and put my coffee down in front of the cushion next to her.

"Knockout," I said, reaching across the table for my mug.

"Right. Not everybody is born lusty, darlin'; some of us have to work damn hard at it." She lifted another piece of cake into her mouth. "You sure you won't have a slice? It's my own recipe, sour cream chocolate chip."

"Too early in the day. Listen, Frieda, it's none of my business, but . . ." I didn't know how to put my question tactfully.

"It's okay, darlin'. I know what I look like."

"But?"

"But why would anybody who was built like that want to become like this? Some damn expensive therapists have asked me the same question. I'll give you my best answer: it's a disguise, okay? Like a kind of hiding."

I lit a cigarette and took a sip of my coffee. I was aware of a shift of feeling, of our being drawn more intimately together. "I stopped smoking for a couple of years back then," I said, indicating the photograph and the Movement buttons. "But I couldn't stick to it."

"Why'd you start again?"

"I like cigarettes."

We laughed together.

"What's after you that you need a disguise?"

"Those were crazy days, weren't they, darlin'? Back when we still believed the future was kind of an ever-improving present, just kicking Nixon around forever. Hey, were you at Mayday?"

I nodded. "Woodstock?"

"Would I have missed it? We're trading secret signs here, like the old Black Power handshake. Right, Malcolm?" She put her plate down on the floor and the dog came up and licked the crumbs. "I found him during the first Mobe, when we attacked the Justice Department and drove John Mitchell off the balcony. Malcolm here is a Movement orphan."

"Was there a particular time, a moment, when you felt it was over?"

"Not really. I mean, I've spent the last four years trying to organize drivers so the companies can't keep fucking us over. Okay, I've been eating to my heart's content since 1975. It's too bad you don't go for big girls, Henry. I got a lot for you."

Her candor caught me by surprise still again. What she was offering I didn't want, but the offer wasn't entirely unwelcome. I almost said to Frieda that there was somebody else but then thought of the necessity of explaining—the thought of Jessica conjured up more unwelcome images—and bit my tongue. An old sixties poster: Don't Just Do Something, Stand There.

Frieda gave me a wry, intimate look. "You're a really good guy, so I'll give you the best answer I know. Love's a two-edged sword. There's really no time now, darlin', to get into it. It wouldn't do for La Jefa to be late for the battle. Let's shove, there'll be plenty more time to rap about this stuff.''

Frieda filled Malcolm's water bowl, slung her shoulder bag with its big Alliance button, and took along an umbrella even though it was, as Peter had said, a glorious day, with blue skies and a light sea breeze.

Seven

Geronimo was already at the demonstration, positioned on the wide, shallow front steps of City Hall facing the plaza. He was standing with his legs spread apart, shouting through a bullhorn, "Cab drivers are being killed on the streets and what is our mayor doing about it? Satisfying her political opportunism out of our pockets."

Nobody was paying much attention to what he was saying because of the sight of an unbroken stream of taxicabs slowly circling City Hall two abreast, their horns honking. There were Yellow Cabs and Checkers; royal-blue-and-white Veterans cabs and red, white, and blue Luxors; beige Metros and orange, fuchsia, lime, ruby, and red cabs; cabs of every stripe and description. They looked like war-painted Indians circling the settlers' covered wagons, and the drivers were not only honking their horns but yipping and shouting slogans and shaking their fists at the indifferent edifice of the city government.

I watched for a while and then slipped away into City Hall, passing beneath the grand rotunda of the elegant marble lobby. City wage slaves hurried from office to office, decimal points in the equation of government that had begun with this magnificent concrete embodiment of a dream of men's worthiness. I went to the registrar's office and looked over the records of recent political contributions, finding some pretty interesting stuff.

When I got back outside, the ungodly racket was still in full voice. I felt a tug at my elbow. Brian Scott, the Checker Cab lawyer, was urging me off to the side of the steps where the din of Geronimo's angry denunciations wasn't so deafening.

"A very vivid display," he said. "Are you going to be meeting with the mayor?"

"Don't know. I think Geronimo and Frieda and a few of the others are going to go up there and demand to see her."

He took off his thick eyeglasses and rubbed them on his tie. "Demands have the effect of putting her back up. She's much more amenable to requests. Shouldn't I come along? Since we're all seeking the same happy results?"

I smiled at him. "Better ask Geronimo, he's a reasonable sort."

At the moment Geronimo, his face flushed and contorted by feeling as well as by the effort to be heard above the din, was screaming through his bullhorn: "We will not be crucified upon a cross of your political ambitions. Do you hear our righteous anger, Abigail?"

"Any resemblance to William Jennings Bryan stops at their both being short and loud," Brian said.

"They're terrified, Brian. Can you imagine what it's like right now to be alone in your taxi in a nasty neighborhood and somebody is flagging you down? If this was just about the medallions, do you think all these drivers would have given up a couple of hours of fares to come down here?"

"Of course."

There was a blessed decline in the noise level. Geronimo had relinquished the bullhorn to another, quieter driver. Flushed and sweating from what was probably the first public speech of his life, he was listening as kibitzers—who constituted the largest single subspecies of the genus taxi driver—filled his ear with praise and advice. Geronimo's eyes were fixed on me and Brian Scott, and there was hatred and suspicion in them. Just then Brian sang out in his loud, raspy voice, "Wiley. Wiley. Over here."

A tall, athletic-looking man responded to Scott's call by changing direction as he came down the stairs. He was wearing an expensively cut gray suit, a pale blue shirt with a white collar clasped by a gold pin, and tasseled black loafers which gleamed. The whole effect he created was one of polish and muscular grace.

"Brian," he said quietly.

"Wiley, good to see you. Wiley, you know Ben Henry? Ben's working with the taxi Alliance, lending them his expertise. Wiley Nottingham."

We leaned across Brian to shake hands. My hand just missed engaging his fully, and my grip was awkwardly weak. Nottingham had long, supple fingers. He took me in with a fast appraisal. I noticed his high cheekbones and almost nonexistent eyebrows, which gave his round handsome face a suggestion of the Oriental.

'Who are the spokespersons for your group?" he asked. "The mayor would like to meet with a small number of your people to see if our differences can't be ironed out."

"You work for the mayor?"

"Day and night." He smiled easily.

"Wiley is her strong right arm," Brian said.

"I'm her deputy in charge of liaising with certain sectors, including Justice."

The taxis were still circling City Hall, their horns complaining. "I'll go tell the steering committee." I crossed the wide staircase, climbing to where Frieda and Geronimo were listening to a husky driver with dangling shirttails who was taking a turn with the bullhorn.

"The mayor's sent down an invitation to meet with the steering committee," I told them.

Geronimo said, "Why didn't they ask *us*?"

I ignored him.

He said something to the driver with the bullhorn, who handed it over to him. "The mayor wants to meet with us," Geronimo shouted through it. "We're going upstairs, but everybody stay here and support us. Solidarity is our only power." He began to hand back the bullhorn but then had an afterthought. "We'll come back and report what she says." He raised a clenched fist over his head.

I led him, Frieda, and two other drivers to where Wiley Nottingham was waiting. As we reached him a strange expression, part surprise and, if I wasn't mistaken, part fear, washed across Frieda's face.

"Something the matter?" I asked her quietly.

"Stage fright, darlin'. What does this sharp dude call himself?"

"Wiley Nottingham, the mayor's strong right arm." In a more audible voice I said to him, "Here we are."

He nodded and turned—abruptly, I thought—and led the way. There was a stiff silence in the elevator. Nottingham used a key to open a door to the mayor's suite of offices, and we emerged from the wide marble corridor into a quiet, carpeted inner passageway paneled in dark wood. He asked us to wait for a moment in a room where three secretaries were working. None of them looked up at us. When he came back he said, "The mayor will see you now." He held open the door.

I realized to my surprise that we were being led into the mayor's private sitting room, not into the larger ceremonial office. The drivers looked awed, and I think one or two of them might have tugged their forelocks in another age. Though it was midday, the heavy drapes were drawn across the one window and lamps were burning. There were several love seats and upholstered chairs, a low coffee table, and tasteful historical prints on the walls. The room was intimate but impersonal. It gave me a spooky feeling because it was the room where Mayor George Moscone had been assassinated. Instinctively I looked for old bloodstains on the carpet, but of course all the furnishings had been changed years since. I was the last one in, and the mayor was standing, shaking hands with each of our group in turn.

"I'm very glad you could come today," she said, offering

a firm hand and a fixed smile. We all stood uneasily and she waited a beat or two before gesturing for us to sit. We sat. She remained standing, leaning on the cane that was her trademark. Everyone knew that she had overcome polio as a child, and since then had surmounted a number of epic or tragic circumstances, including being kidnapped by radical crazies from whom she had escaped. Now she was a shining prospect to be the first woman on a national political ticket. She was a slim, handsome figure in a tailored strawberry suit with wide, padded shoulders and matching pumps. Her nail polish and her lipstick were also perfectly matched, and their color complemented her suit. Her mouth was wide but not generous. There were remarkably few lines in her face for a woman of fifty, an indication not of the surgeon's art but of unbending self-control. No gray at all showed in her honey-colored hair, which was brushed into a medium-short, swept-back executive style. Her eyes, to which your own were magnetically drawn, were a pale green. Abigail Goodman was a redoubtable woman.

She and I had talked before, most recently after the death of the publisher of *The Courier*, a death to which I had been the only witness. Her eyes passed from me to Wiley Nottingham.

"Mr. Henry is working for the Alliance, Mayor." He had read her unspoken question.

"Of course. It's a pleasure to see you again, Ben." The politician's flair for remembering names and faces was no less impressive for being a universal requirement for holding public office.

"Now," she said, still leaning on her cane. "As you know, this administration has proposed to the Police Commission that three hundred new taxicab medallions are urgently required by the City of San Francisco. I want you to know frankly that I haven't retreated from our position one inch. The reasons? The current level of service being provided by your industry is simply not acceptable in a world-class city whose number-one industry is tourism. My office has received an unacceptably high level of complaints from our citizens in outlying neighborhoods about long delays when they need a taxicab. That won't do. Not in the City of San Francisco. I want to hear your input on how we can work together to improve the level of service you are providing.''

Absolutely marvelous. I almost applauded. The way she set up the meeting, the burden was on the drivers to defend their efficiency.

"You're trying to screw us, with all respect, ma'am,'' Geronimo said. "There are drivers out there who work ten- and twelve-hours shifts and hardly bring home enough for their families to live on. Now you want to increase the competition on the streets by forty percent. I've got some figures here,'' he said, turning the pages on a clipboard.

"John,'' she said, both her hands on the handle of her cane, "you had better understand right now, before you go any further, that the matter of the new medallions is now before the Police Commission. The Police Commission, not the mayor's office, is the appropriate authority. Any problem you have with it should properly be brought to the commissioners, and I can assure you of a full and fair hearing for your point of view. What we can productively talk about today is your input on improving taxi service. Frankly, my concern is, one, that there are people in our neighborhoods, the elderly, the handicapped, the chronically ill, who need better taxi service. And two, that it is a matter of civic pride that we live up to our world-class reputation as a can-do city when the eyes of the nation are on us this summer.''

"The handicapped? The elderly?'' This was the husky driver who had tucked in his shirttails. "Hey, excuse me, lady, but who do you think is ferrying them around now? Hey, there isn't a driver out there who doesn't know where every kidney dialysis machine in the city is. You know how many times a day we fold a wheelchair into our trunks, and those suckers weigh a ton, lady, and walk some old bag of sticks up two flights of stairs for a dime tip, which is damn nice of her, too, because with the benefits you people pay she can be damn lucky to eat all week. So don't tell us about the handicapped and the elderly.''

"Steve's right," Frieda said. "But maybe we should talk about Greg White. And Al Dwiri.''

"Yeah, and Frank Iancini," said Steve. "He was a buddy of mine. What about the drivers whose throats are getting slit, lady? What are you doing about that?''

Abigail sat down in a captain's chair, picked up a telephone, and pushed a button. It must have been a direct line that rang on a desk in the Hall of Justice, because a second later she said, "Good morning, Chief. I have the steering committee of the taxicab drivers' Alliance with me. They're very naturally expressing concern about what your department is doing to protect their safety.''

She listened for a moment.

"I think they will be very pleased to learn about the task force, Chief. And I want you to know that the city is offering a five-thousand-dollar reward. I have a discretionary fund for situations that fall within these parameters. Thank you, Chief.'' She put down the phone. Watching her was like watching a sound-bite: her transactions were timed and trimmed for the exigencies of Action George's crowd.

"Chief Riley informs me his department has set up a task force to concentrate solely and exclusively on apprehending the person or persons responsible for these attacks. I'm glad to be able to tell you that the city is also offering a reward of five thousand dollars for information leading to the conviction of whoever killed Mr. White and the others. Mr. Nottingham will be representing me personally at the funeral.'' She propped the cane under her chin with both hands resting on its handle. "We're as concerned as you are about this matter.''

"Wasn't the reward ten thousand dollars for whoever shot that banker up in your neighborhood a couple of months ago?" Steve asked.

"Ma'am," said Geronimo, "we appreciate that. But that's got nothing to do with putting three hundred new cabs out there. We're not going to let you get away with that, your convention be damned."

She pointed a sharp, red-tipped index finger at him. "I don't respond to threats, John."

"Nonviolent, peaceful protest is our right," he said, starting to get excited.

"Hey, we're scared, lady," Steve said. "And you're stomping us when we're down. Maybe the only way we can get you to pay attention is if every cab in the city just happens to run out of gas down at the airport the day your convention starts."

"Let me remind you, Steve, that under the terms of the chauffeur's license issued to you by the city and county of San Francisco, the Police Department can terminate any taxicab driver who doesn't perform his duties. You would do well to remember that." Her pale green eyes traveled around the room, resting on each driver's face in turn.

Frieda hauled herself up with a grunt of effort from a low love seat. "I guess if that's the best you can do, we'd better hit the road. C'mon, you guys. I almost forgot, though, Madam Mayor, we brought this along for your friend Sally Bender. Compliments of the Alliance."

She held out a rolled-up umbrella to the mayor, who had no choice but to take it.

Eight

Wiley Nottingham fell in beside me as we left. "Why don't you come around to see me about six on Friday?" he said, barely moving his thin lips. He didn't turn to face me when he spoke; nobody else was intended to hear. Cloak-and-dagger. Not to disappoint him, I replied with a barely perceptible dip of my chin.

A honey blonde in a white blouse with a bow at her neck popped her head out of an office door opposite. She was holding a stack of papers. "Hurry up, Wiley. She's starting in a minute. We need you to check out the release." She had the purposeful chipperness of a detergent commercial.

"Goodbye, thanks for coming," he said to our little group. He extended his hand to each of us in turn, although when Frieda went by she ducked her head and ignored his hand.

I asked the squeaky-clean girl with the Abigail lookalike hairdo for a copy of the release.

"Sure, I guess that's okay," she said.

I skimmed it, picking out the words "task force" and the figure $5,000. That was why the mayor had chosen to meet with us in her private sitting room instead of her big office, which was a more intimidating room, and where it seemed a press conference was about to begin. Her little display of calling Chief Alphonso Riley had been a sham within a sham. The woman was a fiend for detail.

61

Nottingham met my eye and shrugged. He looked amused. I considered whether to suggest to the steering committee that they should gate-crash the press conference. Wiley would feel grateful if I let it slide, but my real consideration was that when the mayor started to lie—lying was one of only two possible reasons for holding a press conference, the other being boasting—Geronimo would probably lose his cool, and I didn't think it would help anything for Geronimo to be seen ranting at the mayor on the evening news. How had I become a baby-sitter to this schmuck?

Just then I saw Nellie Flynn hurrying along, his thin, rounded shoulders bent as if he were walking into the face of a gale. I hailed him.

He turned, squinted myopically, and started toward us. "Yo," he said, and then to Nottingham: "Started yet, Wiley?"

"You've got a minute," I told him. "Wiley has to check over the release. How's the old prophet-maker? You know the leadership of the Alliance?" I made introductions.

"Been meeting with the mayor?" Nellie's spiral pad was out of his jacket pocket, and he was flipping pages with a knobbly hand that held a Bic.

"We walked out on her," Geronimo asserted.

"Did you?" Nellie started to write.

"The mayor just brought us up here to manipulate us," Geronimo said. "She has no sympathy for drivers or any other working people. Nothing she had to say changed our minds. She's trying to crucify us on the cross of her own political ambitions." Nothing inflates a small ego as much as self-quotation.

"I see." Nellie was scribbling, a barely tolerant expression on his shrewd red face. "Gonna strike?"

I turned away and held up six fingers for six o'clock Friday so Nottingham could see. Then I led Frieda aside. Nottingham watched us with a peculiar expression before he abruptly went back into the mayor's suite, closing the door behind him.

"I have to go," I told her, bending over. She was a foot shorter than I. "The whole thing was a setup. She was trying to get you out of the way so the press didn't talk to you before she had her say. Listen, I loved the umbrella."

"I got a dozen of 'em, darlin'. People leave them in the cab. How do you think it went?"

"It didn't do any harm. I'll call you later, we can do a postmortem. Here, here's the press release she's giving out."

Frieda took it in a pudgy hand with deep creases at the knuckles. "Check. Listen, there's something I've got to tell you."

"We'll talk later. I'm in a rush now."

"Okay, it can wait. Okay. Later, 'gator."

I was old enough to know I was supposed to say, "While, 'dile," and too old to say it. "See ya, toots, " I said instead.

A mob of reporters was leaving the Homicide Division when I reached the fourth floor of the Hall of Justice, among them Action George and his crew. He looked at me, trying to place me, but I didn't stop on my way past. The gang of scriveners gathered like flies buzzing over a dog's calling card created a sense of crisis as much as the killings themselves did. Reporters, especially the television ones, began to believe that they were as much a part of a big story as the cops, the murderer, and the victims. The arrogance of it annoyed me, but really, they were no different from anybody else: even the shyest person is the hero of his own internal novel.

Miss Lipschultz was at her desk, barring the door to the squad room. There were a lot like her in the anterooms of the Hall, women of a certain age, single, sympathetic, shaped into one form of bitterness or another by being on call to a succession of cops whose wives, snug and secure in suburbia tending broods of kids, couldn't encompass the urgent excitements their husbands needed to spill. Miss Lipschultz won nothing but consolation prizes.

"Browder's expecting me," I told her. "Busy morning?"

"Just the press," she said with exquisite boredom. "I'll tell him you're here." She picked up a phone and pressed a button. "Ben Henry to see you. Okay. He says to go on back." She turned away from me, slipped on a headset, and bent her crimson talons back over her typewriter.

The linoleum in the Homicide squad room was scraped and worn, and the windows had factory panes. None of the detectives looked up from their newspapers, their talk, their case files, as I went to Browder's desk, and none of them missed my arrival. It was a room of men who see without seeming to look.

"Where were you this morning?" Browder said.

"I'm sorry, Jim. I had to see the mayor. I got here as soon as I could."

"He had to see the mayor, Jimmy." This was Browder's partner, Corelli, a thin detective with a long, sagging, doleful face. "For crissake, Jimmy, you can understand that, the mayor."

"She asked after you, Corelli. She said she hoped you were eating right, that there's got to be a problem with an Italian of your rank who's all skin and bones."

"That was a joke, Jimmy," Corelli said. "Ben Henry, he's got that dry kind of wit. You got to listen very careful to what the man says."

"We want a statement." Browder handed me a pad.

"You want me to write it?"

"It's the pad, Jimmy. 'At's how he scoped it. Guy should have been a cop, you know what I mean?"

"We're going down the caf. Be back in fifteen minutes," Browder said. "Go ahead, use my typewriter there."

They started for the door. They were exactly the same sawed-off height.

"Oh, Corelli, you don't mind if it's grammatical, do you?"

They shook their heads like two marionettes on the same set of strings as they went out. I began pecking out what had happened the night before on Browder's old Royal upright, impeded by an *s* key that stuck whenever I hit it.

When Browder returned he was alone. He read what I had written, slipping on glasses with black frames and wobbly earpieces. When he finished reading, he took them off and put them back in the handkerchief pocket of his jacket.

"I don't want you sticking your nose into an official investigation." He ran a palm over a stubbly cheek. I didn't suppose he had had time to go home since I had last seen him.

"You find out anything about Greg White?"

There was a long pause before he said, "What, like?"

"Was he a gambler? Al Dwiri was in hock to Chris Manchuco. I talked to Manchuco and he told me more or less to stay out of the Mission."

"Typical. No. But Manchuco don't have the garbanzos for this kind of work."

"Find a weapon?"

"That's police information." After a pause he rubbed his eyes with his knuckles. "Nah."

"Prints? Witnesses? Anything?"

"If we did I wouldn't tell you. What we got is a geographical pattern, that's about it. I mean, how do you find a screw-loose psychopath? Two ways." He held up a flat index finger with grime under the nail. "One, a snitch. Remember Zebra? Anthony Carter? That was my case. Called me from a paybox in Oakland. We got out there, it must have been ninety degrees, he was wearing a fur hat and a tuxedo. Two, dumb luck. Like they took down the Son of Sam in New York on a parking ticket. I don't know, I want you to stay out of our hair, that's all. And let me know if you hear anything I should."

"What about the Aleph Mem Tof? You think it means he's Jewish?"

He shook his head. "Got a couple of shrinks working up a psychological profile, they don't think so. Prophet of Doom's pretty close to it, according to them. Can you beat it? These guys want all the attention, they think they got the power, a lot of 'em are pretty bright. It's like a fucking guessing game, he's showing us he's smarter than we are.''

"How come taxi drivers, do you think?"

Browder lifted his palms. "Who can tell? A grudge? We're checking out drivers who the companies fired, people who filed complaints against cabbies.''

Corelli returned, smiling, if you could call the malicious pleasure on his face a smile.

"The computer downstairs kicked out a likely. Leroy Edwards is back on the street. He was released from Folsom in August. Went down for a holdup, a taxi holdup."

"Edwards? He's never done anybody, has he?" Browder said.

"The cabbie testified. Leroy's brothers paid a call on him, but the cabbie went in the box anyway.''

Browder was shaking his head. "The Edwards family's only contribution to San Francisco is raising the crime rate. Leroy can't make change for a dime, and he's the brains of the brothers. Olive Mem Tof is way too deep for him." Browder's tone was dismissive, complaining. Their partnership worked like a longtime marriage, a constant low-level bickering, like one mind arguing with itself. At the same time he was telling Corelli why his idea was no good, Browder was closing files and preparing to start looking for Leroy Edwards.

I got up.

"One more thing," Browder said. He wagged his finger at me. "Be careful out there."

"You like *Hill Street Blues*, huh?"

"It stinks. My kids watch it."

Nine

Six o'clock Friday I parked at a meter outside City Hall. Across Polk Street in the plaza the pigeons and gulls were murmuring and cawing their evening songs. The sun was in the western sky and City Hall cast a broad shadow across the reflecting pool. I had made no progress in finding out anything more about who was murdering cab drivers, but I had seen Mel Dropo, who had pelted me with half-hearted threats and, less expectedly, with a check. It made me suspicious to be paid so promptly.

I was suspicious, too, about what Wiley Nottingham wanted, arranging to meet me almost clandestinely. He made me wait only a minute before he came out of his office, slipping into a gray linen sports jacket lined in maroon satin. He was a strikingly handsome man with a fine round skull crowned with a short frizz of hair.

"Where do you want to talk? You care? There's a bar across the street might be okay. I don't usually drink, but Friday afternoon, what the hell, huh?"

We went out side by side. He was a shade shorter than I was, and took the steps two at a time with effortless athleticism. I didn't like the smell of his cologne—I was strictly an Ivory Soap man myself, 99 and 44 one hundredths pure— and most cologne smelled to me like chemistry labs. His was distinctly unpleasant, but I have a cynical nose.

"You like games?" he asked as we turned into McAllister Street. A lawyer named Hall McAllister had bribed a city commissioner with a bottle of champagne back in 1849 to have a thoroughfare named after him, and eventually City Hall had been built on a street whose very name was corrupt.

"I play a little basketball, I get out to Candlestick, that's about it."

Nottingham laughed. "No, I mean like word associations, that kind of jazz. Here, I'll give you a city, you give me the first thing you associate with it. Ready?"

"Shoot."

"L.A."

"Freeway."

"Right. New York."

"Money."

"Gotcha. Chicago."

"Love."

"Love?"

"I saw a man/ He danced with his wife/ In Chicago."

"Okay. You from Chicago, huh?"

"What about you?"

"No, wait a minute. Still playing. Boston."

"Yastrzemski."

"San Francisco."

That stopped me cold. I couldn't think of anything to say. It's hardest to be facile about what you know best.

"Know what most people associate with us? Kooks. You dig? That's our problem, that's what we've got to overcome."

Wiley's vocabulary was hip and breezy but his diction was almost stilted. The careful diction combined with the hip talk suggested a tension or a pose.

The bar was packed with civil servants having an after-work drink, and we had to wait for the waitress to come over to take our orders.

"Hiya, Wiley," she said. "The usual? And your friend?"

I ordered a Beck's.

"A Beck's and a double gin and ginger," she said.

"The Kook City image is our problem," he continued when the pale gold drink was in his big hand. "You take the national media, now, they love my boss's profile. We have requests pending from *Time, The New York Times, Newsweek*, the three networks, and cable—you name it, they all want to do her. She's running the only damn city in the country with a budget surplus, she's pretty *and* tough, and she's some kind of hero. The cane helps, too, strikes the FDR bell, courageous and compassionate. She's high profile. And this is the year for a woman on the national ticket; you can smell it on the wind. Our only problem is kooks. Prophet of goddamn Doom."

"So the way you see it, Wiley, this creep who's killing drivers is a real impediment to the mayor's political future?"

The irony wasn't lost on him. "Whoa, hey. Is wringing my hands and beating my breast going to make any difference to those poor bastards? If you don't want to hear what I have to say, tell me; we'll just finish our drinks and be on our merry way."

"The way the mayor handled the Alliance on Wednesday wasn't exactly reassuring."

"She doesn't bend easily, that's why I'm useful. A little flexibility in the steel makes building bridges possible."

"Okay, go ahead," I told him.

"It wouldn't be so bad if we weren't hosting the convention, but there's ten thousand press coming here."

"Maybe the cops'll catch him soon."

"They don't have a clue," he said. "You ready for another?" He held up his empty glass and caught the waitress's eye. " 'Cept that Hebrew jazz."

"You know about that?"

"The chief doesn't fart without my boss picking up the phone and asking him what's that funny smell. I'm liaising on this one."

"Well, what's it supposed to mean?"

"What is?"

"Aleph Mem Tof. Truth."

"Means there's a rabbi in the woodpile."

I laughed.

He grinned and finished off his second gin and ginger in a long swallow.

"I haven't talked to Browder in a couple of days," I said. "They find Leroy Edwards yet?"

He shook his head. "So tell me, about these cab drivers. Who's the real power? I had a gut feeling about that little fat gal, what's her name?"

"Frieda, Frieda Mishkin."

He looked at me intently with his brown, limpid eyes, holding the stare for a long time, as if waiting for me to say more. When I didn't, he smiled. "She's the bright one."

"So?" Good intelligence or good instincts?

"So I thought perhaps we could cook up a little mutual aid."

"You and me?"

"Who else but Nelse. Hey, hold it, wait a minute, keep it right there. I have to whiz." On his way, he leaned over the waitress, saying something from close by her ear that made her laugh. He wasn't yet back at our table when she brought around another round of drinks.

"Well, what do you say?" he asked when he had returned.

"You better spell it out for me, Wiley. What do you want."

"Okay, the way I see it, my boss is going overboard here. Three hundred cabs are way too many, I understand that, and so do the sensible people on the Police Commission. I've talked to a few of them and they're not going to vote for that. But I'll tell you something else, the idea wasn't entirely Abigail's. John Lemon and his crowd are hungry for more medallions, never mind what they tell the drivers. You and I are pretty well situated to know what's going on on all sides of this one. Nobody wins if they strike when the convention's on. The drivers lose all that loose money and earn a lot of bad will. Last damn thing the city needs is a taxi strike *and* a Prophet of Doom on the loose, making it seem like Abigail isn't in control. You can see how badly that would play.''

"So you think that between us we can restrict the number of new medallions, and trade enough information to keep everybody from getting unduly excited? I don't see anything wrong with that, Wiley.''

"You're okay. That stuff they put around about you being a maverick is some bullshit, the way we said when I was outgrowing short pants.''

"Where was that?''

He ignored the question. After a long swallow he said, "You've got to understand, man, we're in this for real. I'm talking four years in the D. of C., maybe eight. Maybe,'' he went on, leaning closer, "just maybe sixteen. I'm talking about the *back* seat of a limo.''

"Just so you understand, Wiley, I don't care whether Abigail Goodman becomes Vice President or not. I want to find the killer, and I want to keep the drivers from being screwed to the floor. If you can help me there, I'll do what I can for you.''

"To it.'' He lifted his glass.

I gave him an old Scot's toast in return. "May we spend a half hour in heaven before the devil hears we're dead.'' Our glasses clinked.

"Hey,'' Wiley said, "you like tacos?''

"I'm not really hungry.''

"No, no. The wife is making tacos and I was supposed to be home an hour ago. C'mon with me, she makes a great taco.''

I had no better plans.

"I tell you what,'' Wiley said. "Let's have one more, and then we'll boogie on down to Mrs. N.'s taco house. How's that sound?''

The world was taking on the soft golden glow of Wiley's

double gin and gingers. I had lost track of how many rounds we had put away.

"You always been hungry for the back seat of a limo?" I asked.

"No, no." He was solemn, giving the question careful consideration. "I have a kid who's not well, you'll see. It changes you, you know? My son was dealt a busted hand, I don't want him to go through the things I had to, he's got it tough enough. You married?"

"No. Was." I was falling in with his mood, feeling maudlin.

"Yeah. Well, here's the thing, okay? It doesn't matter if you remember the past, it doesn't forget you."

"No, it doesn't."

"Damn right. When I caught on with Abigail, I had a lot of making up to do. I like it when guys who can buy and sell me call me Mr. Nottingham. I'm trusting you, talking this way. You're not going to do me dirty, are you?"

"No, why would I?"

Ten

Wiley drove a little uncertainly on our way out to his place. The house was at the end of a cul-de-sac bordering on the Presidio. The street had a quiet, woodsy feel. When he unlocked the front door and stepped inside, he whistled a greeting. A boy's voice cried out, "Daddy!"

The kid came rolling out of the kitchen in an electric wheelchair. His arms and legs were emaciated, and his head was supported by a leather strap around his forehead. He rolled up to Wiley, who bent over and mussed his hair and chucked him under his chin.

"You been a good boy today?" Wiley asked him. The boy beamed with pleasure. His muscular control wasn't good and he made involuntary movements. "This is Mr. Henry. My son, Jackie." I said hi.

Wiley's wife came into the hall, where we were still standing. "Hello, hon," she said. "Supper's ready."

"This is my friend Ben," Wiley said. "Got enough tacos to go around?"

Mrs. Nottingham, who was nearly as tall as her husband, offered a long, slim, warm hand. "Ann Nottingham," she said. "We'd be pleased if you would join us. From the look of things, Wiley might never have found his way home without your help." She smiled indulgently at Wiley, who was down on his knees in front of Jackie's wheelchair, engaged in horseplay that had the boy laughing with delight.

73

"What?" said Wiley.

"I told Ben there was always a place at our table for somebody who brings you home."

Ann Nottingham was still smiling, and her tone remained playful, but there was a subtext of feeling to her remark that I read more clearly in a tiny, irritated toss of Wiley's head than in anything she had revealed with her banter. The silence that followed was a tick too long for comfort.

"He wanted to wait up for you," Ann said. "Didn't you, honey?"

"Daddy," Jackie said, his head lolling as he spoke the arduously formed words, "will you read me a bedtime comic?"

"We bought some new ones today," the boy's mother said. "Over at that place on Clement. He's only read them himself three times already."

The boy looked imploringly at his father and made sounds of undisguised longing that were enough to break your heart.

"You get the new Teenage Mutant Ninja Turtles?" Wiley asked, and the knowledge of his son's world implied by the question added a few inches to his stature in my estimation. Jackie almost fell out of his chair, nodding with excitement and spinning his wheels in a half circle as he started toward a lift attached to the banister leading upstairs.

"Be a minute, is all," Wiley said to me. And to Ann: "Ben's drinking beer." As he climbed upstairs beside the rising wheelchair he asked Jackie, "How'd the swim therapy go today?"

Ann led the way and I followed her through the dining room, where two places were set, and on to the kitchen. She had wonderful posture, a straight back, square shoulders, and that long-striding way of walking that showed she had once received training as a model. It hadn't surprised me that Wiley was married to a black woman; in fact, when I had first seen her, it was as if I had been expecting it. The interracial marriage offered an insight into the way his precise, clipped pronunciation and his hip phrases seemed to contradict each other. Wiley had spent a lot of time, I now guessed, among educated black people, not a few of whom had two distinct ways of talking—one for Whitey's world and another for their own.

Ann took a cold Elephant Malt Liquor from the refrigerator and poured most of it into a glass mug kept in the freezer. The kitchen was spotless—it was my curse to forever be judging the cleanliness of every home I walked into—and very capably made. The cabinetry was wormy old pine, two walls were exposed brick, the French doors let onto a walled garden that was lit by fixtures hidden among the shrubs and flowers, and the appliances had a sleek, understated designer-conscious look. In the middle of the room was a long butcher-block table with white-painted bentwood chairs around it. I wondered at the formality of the laid places in the dining room and why the Nottinghams didn't eat in the kitchen on nights when they expected to dine alone.

"I hope you don't mind tacos," Ann said when she put my beer down on the butcher-block table and sat down herself in front of a half-empty glass of white wine and soda.

"It smells great," I said sincerely. "Look, I'm sorry about keeping Wiley out so late at the bar."

This time it was Ann who gave that involuntary little shake of the head, gazing at me with enormous eyes. She was a beautiful woman with lovely manners, secure in her impeccable kitchen, and yet I couldn't shake the feeling of tension I had been aware of ever since I had entered her domain.

"You weren't responsible," she said, meaning, I suppose, that I didn't have to pretend that it was I who had kept us drinking past suppertime and the point of sobriety. She crossed her legs and picked up her wineglass. "The malt liquor is what you wanted?"

I swallowed from the chilled mug. "Wonderful. It's very nice of you to invite me. I suppose it must be disconcerting having me show up unexpectedly like this. I'm really sorry to intrude, but Wiley was so extravagant in his praise for your tacos I just couldn't resist."

"That's very nice. There's plenty to go around." As she said it, I knew it was true, there was plenty, and for the same reason the places were laid in the dining room and not in the homier kitchen—it was not unusual for Wiley to come home late, loaded and with company in tow. "You work in City Hall, too?" Ann asked.

"No. I'm working with some people who are negotiating with the mayor, and Wiley and I were just getting our heads together. Wiley and Jackie are really lovely to watch together."

"They are," she agreed. "Jackie's a love gift, most people don't understand, they think he's a burden, but Wiley and I know the rewards as well as the hardships." She rose and put on a white oven glove imprinted with red ducks and checked on the supper, which was keeping warm. When she opened the oven door, the aroma gusted into the kitchen. I took a long swallow of my beer.

"I expect you work often with Wiley," Ann said, pronouncing the *t* in often.

"No, actually we only just met. At a meeting in the mayor's office. It's obvious she puts a lot of trust in Wiley, though."

Ann nodded. "You know, we both fell in love with Abigail Goodman the first time we ever met her back in Chicago. Wiley and I were serving on a planning group for the Special Olympics and Abigail made a speech. She's got a real genuine interest in physically challenged kids. We talked for hours and hours, and the next morning she called our hotel room at seven o'clock and offered Wiley a job out here. It was truly amazing, Wiley had been on the staff of the Police Review Board in St. Louis, you know, and I mean, the job out here paid so much better and had so much more responsibility. It was just breathtaking, one evening we went to a planning session and before breakfast Wiley was being asked to be deputy mayor of San Francisco. We're both really grateful to the mayor. The next time you visit I'll be sure to show you the proclamation in Jackie's room, he was the poster boy for the Special Olympics when they held it out here last year. The mayor insisted."

I had finished my beer, and without bothering to ask, Ann poured me another one. She checked the oven again. "Excuse me a minute, will you?" she said.

"Sure." She left and I heard her going upstairs. I sat still, straining to hear more. Minute after minute went by. Finally she returned.

"I think we'll have to start without Wiley," she said. "He's not feeling too well and I told him he had better go to bed. I hope you don't mind?"

"Ann," I said, "let me tell you the truth. I ate supper just before I met Wiley. I'm an early eater." I yawned spontaneously: my mind is always amazing me with its readiness to conspire in my lies. "And I'm really tired, too. Could I take a rain check on the tacos without putting you out?"

Ann was so clearly grateful that it took us only two or three more polite mistruths to get to the point where I stood up and she walked with me to the front door. She had enough on her hands without me to be fed and entertained.

Despite whatever problems they had, the Nottinghams had both made me feel welcome in their home, and I left regretting having at first sized Wiley up as glib and unscrupulous.

Eleven

"It's madness out there, I kid you not," said a driver named Bob with blond streaks and two tiny gold studs piercing his left earlobe. He was waiting near the dispatch cage with a couple of other Checker drivers whose shifts were about ready to begin. I had come to the yard looking for Frieda, and had decided to take a taxi out myself.

A driver they called Hawk because of his aquiline nose and rapacious appetite for an argument made a disgusted sound. "My wife says lay off until they catch him. I says to her, 'The kids need new clothes for school, so what are we going to do for money? Live on *your* salary?'"

"Wait, no," said Bob, who had a point he was still trying to make. "You know the blind lady who sees all the plays?"

"Mrs. Ritchie, 411 29th Avenue," said Hawk. He had a paperback edition of Hegel's *Philosophy of History* jammed into the back pocket of his worn polyester pants.

"That's the one, right. Well, I catch her at the Marines Memorial Theater last night, she saw a play."

"Listened," Hawk said, running his palm over his bald pate. "She can't see."

Bob, who had a baby face and a two-day stubble, wasn't going to be put off by Hawk's dialectical obstinacy. "I rode her home, seven ten on the meter and a buck tip, and right up the block some guy is out there in the deep avenues flagging

78

me. I mean, do you get flagged at Twenty-ninth and Anza at eleven-thirty? No way, right? He tells me he's locked out of his place, he has to go get his keys from his mother out in Oakland, Fruitvale somewhere, and come on back.''

There was an almost imperceptible settling in by our little congregation. Taxi stories, the small tales of the trade. It made you wonder what drolleries morticians exchanged when they talked shop.

"Iss good damn ride," said a third driver, a Russian émigré named Boris who had a slow, habitual smile and always knew whom you should go see to get a ticket fixed, or a cut-rate pair of Italian shoes.

"Forty bucks easy," said Bob. "Only it gave me the shakes. I mean, do I want to take this guy out to who-knows-where Oakland? Flagging me down in the deep avenues late? This could be the one. I can't get it out of my head."

The question Bob was posing, and that Hawk and Boris were embroidering, was the real meaning of the Prophet of Doom killings out on the streets: What is the value of your own life?

Hawk jammed his hands into the pockets of a baby-blue windbreaker. "So?"

"I made him sit up next to me where I can watch him and I rode with a hand on my tire iron, I've been keeping it down next to my feet. But I'll tell you, it's not worth it. The whole damn ride my stomach's like Mount St. Helens. I drop him at his mother's, that was it. Bob, I say to myself, let him get an Oakland cab home. On a night like this the best thing is to bend her over and take her in."

"He tip you?" Hawk asked.

"A deuce," Bob said. All the best taxi stories end the same way—with a good tip.

"Reagan. If he doesn't close the mental hospitals do you think the streets would be like this?"

"Reagan iss a feather in history," said Boris. "All he cares iss no taxes."

"What a job," Bob said. "Why do I do it?"

"It's not a job, that's what you don't understand," said Hawk. "It's just a way of making money."

"You want to know, yess?" Boris said to Bob. "I tell you. Iss like guy in bar telling bartender hiss troubles. So bartender tells, 'Talk with my machine, okay?' When guy gives money in, machine sayss to him, 'Hello, what iss IQ?' Guy sayss one hundred and fivty, yess? Machine sayss, 'How come iss more we know all the time less and less we believe in God?' Very interesting to discuss when machine sayss after, 'You want talk like thiss more, another fivty cents.' The guy gives money. Again machine sayss, 'Hello, what iss IQ?' One hundred thiss time. Machine sayss, 'You think 49ers go to Super Bowl?' After football talk when time iss over, guy puts more fivty cents. IQ iss fivty. Machine sayss nothing, you know. Guy waits. Machine sayss, 'So how's things in taxi business?' Yess?"

Bob and I laughed but Hawk was shaking his head vehemently. "The way they run this place is just like the entire country. What's supposed to be the difference between that deformed little freak Lemon who needs electroshock to figure out what's going on and the trained cadaver in the White House who's been bombed on thorazine for the past fifteen years?"

Bob said, "Lemon's wife don't call him 'Daddy.' "

We all laughed again. Boris smiled a big smile. "Fear," he said. It seemed to apply to nothing and everything, and our little cluster melted away, each of us joining another grouping of drivers or standing alone. I saw John Geronimo nearby and went over to him. He had a plastic protector in his shirt pocket with four pens and a tire gauge clipped to it, and he was holding his taxi bag and a clipboard.

"Seen Frieda?" I asked him.

"What's it to you?" His face was red and his answer was thick with resentment.

"What the hell? What's the matter?"

"I saw you palling it up with Brian Scott and that pimp from the mayor's office over at City Hall." He fished a Philip Morris from a pack wedged in behind the pens. "I think you're a goddamn spy."

The funny thing was that as soon as he said it I felt a familiar furtiveness. Geronimo was right without having any idea of what he was right about. I was a spy by nature: reporter, front-seat eavesdropper, and now paid Question Asker, everything I did was a form of spying. But I was not a traitor.

"It's not true, John," I said. "I'm not a spy." It was the truth, but only so far as he was able to understand it. My ambivalence made me wonder if it was possible to utter a single sentence that was wholly truthful. The answer was maybe.

Geronimo clicked open a Zippo. The flame gave off a gas odor. "She's coming in later," he said, and walked away from me.

Geronimo was a fool, but his accusation kept resonating through my thoughts, and when I took a cab out a little while later I was angry and lonely. Angry at whom? Not that putz Geronimo. At Jessica? Why hadn't she called or written? Maybe she was over there falling back in love with her husband. But really it was myself I was fed up with. Undercover, undershmuver, call it what you want, here I was behind the wheel again. Maybe grubbing out a living in a taxi was where I really belonged after all and where I would end up, a pitiable old man sitting in line outside the Mark Hopkins on a slow Saturday night in winter hoping for an airport ride.

My only company was the dispatch radio, and the monitor which I set to the police band. I drove slowly around the town, passing up flags and licking my wounds. Gradually I headed the taxi toward the south end of the city, where the drivers had been killed. I had an appointment in the morning with a rabbi because I thought there was more to Aleph Mem Tof than anybody had yet understood. The police band was broadcasting the usual effluvia of a San Francisco night. A bar fight. A hit-and-run. A john who had been rolled by a prostitute and her pimp. A prowler. A break-in at a warehouse. An incident at Bayshore and Cortland involving a taxi. I made a quick U-turn and headed that way, my stomach churning with sudden anxiety, and my thoughts, blessedly, wrenched free of myself.

I arrived just behind a prowl car as it pulled up near a taxi stopped under a mercury vapor streetlamp, a Metro cab. The vapor lamp was a sign of an urban danger zone; it turned the street pale and spooky. I was full of dread, but when I reached the cop car I saw that the cab driver was standing in the street, apparently unharmed. It was Joe Bryant, the fat man who had been shouting at Browder the night Greg White was killed. Bryant had a pronounced chin chiseled into heavy jowls, and no neck. I followed the cops toward him. Their guns were unholstered.

"Which way did he go?" one of the cops asked.

"He didn't go anywhere," said Bryant in a foghorn voice. "He's never going anywhere again."

The cop peered inside the taxi. "My God. What happened here?"

"Hey, you," the second cop shouted at me. "Get back away."

I just had time to see into the cab. A man, or what had been a man, was slumped over in the front seat. What remained of his head was resting on the meter. All that was left of him from the neck up was a pulverized mass of gore; it looked as if his head had been crushed beneath the foot of a giant. His topcoat, the seat, the dashboard, and the windows were all soaked with blood. The meter clicked.

"Old Ralph is sure going to be put out," Bryant said with icy irony. "He's going to have one hell of a job cleaning this cab up."

"I asked you, what happened here?" The cop was scream-ing. A greenhorn.

"This nigger tried to hold me up," bellowed Bryant. "Last mistake he ever made. Nobody's going to shoot or slice Joe Bryant, that's not my fate."

"What the hell did you do to him?"

"Shot him once close up with a little .41 Magnum with a lead bullet. Ever see so much blood? Well, you fellas know all about it; you get them in the head the blood's thicker than any place else." He reached in and wrenched the dead man half out of his taxi.

"Hey, stop it! Hey!"

Bryant paid no attention to the young cop's frantic com-mand. He yanked the corpse all the way into the gutter. "You bastard, you picked the wrong target tonight," he said with spiteful relish.

The cop pushed him hard up against the cab. "You're under arrest," he screamed.

"Calm down. I'm not under arrest. This jig tried to rob me, I told you. If they try to rob me they're on their own. He put his life on the limb for what I got in my pocket."

"How do I know he tried to rob you? Where's his weapon?"

Bryant put a heavy black boot under the body before the cop could react, and kicked the dead man over onto his back. A small pistol clattered against the pavement.

"Hey, you, scram. Go on, before I fucking run you in," the second cop shouted at me. I went back to my cab and waited. After a while a metallic silver Porsche arrived. A very tall, impeccably dressed black detective emerged. In-spector Franklin Delano Roosevelt Pressix. In the confusion of ambulance attendants, cops, coroner's deputies, and gawk-ers I edged closer again.

Joe Bryant was explaining to Pressix with a shrewd, hard grin what had happened, gesturing with hands that were small and unlined, strangely childlike hands. "You're not going to find me in some back alley with my throat cut because some nigger wants a few dollars."

Pressix's large, intimidating face was utterly impassive, a sign that he was seething with anger. Very quietly he said, "You refer to him as the robber." He turned to a uniformed cop. "Take him downtown and hold him there for me."

When things had calmed down and most of the vehicles and people had departed as swiftly as they had arrived, I went up to Pressix. His mocha face looked a sickly greenish purple in the vapor light.

"Jus' what I need to make a perfect night. Super snoop." We had tangled in the past but ended up understanding each other.

"God, he's ugly," I said. "I mean deep-down ugly, uglier than that poor soul with his face shot off. Bryant makes me feel ashamed to be a human."

Pressix nodded. "Prob'ly he think he's some kind of hero. What Joe is is one of the nonpeople, not important to his self, not to nobody. Killing this one make him what he want to be, not a fat old ugliness nobody care nuthin' 'bout. Make him feel a little better. He done it couple times before, and got away with it. Victim always seem to have a weapon, never any witness around."

"And this time?"

"This time he ovuhstepped. That one there is Leroy Edwards."

Now I understood. "So Bryant was playing vigilante."

"Wasn't no game. Ah'm gawna nail him so hard he gawna wish he was Edwards. Son of a bitch been hangin' 'round downtown all week. Know what he told me? Told me, 'I did you people a favor. You should thank me.' "

I took out a cigarette and offered one to Pressix. It looked no bigger than a matchstick in his hand. "You got to hand him one thing anyhow, he found Edwards quicker than we could." Pressix exhaled loudly. "Sumthin' in the air, this our third 187 tonight."

"Fear," I said, echoing Boris.

"Sumthin'. How'd you get here so quick, sonny?"

I explained.

"Your good friend Corelli said you bein' a nuisance like always. Be a good boy now, go on home before you get in trouble." He shook his head. "You know what your trouble is? You persistent as a Jehovah's Witness and jus' as welcome."

Twelve

I was beneath the Division street overpass on my way back to the Checker yard when I was given a start by a sudden scream. It was impossible to tell at first where it came from because of the echo chamber created by the roadbed above. I slowed down and leaned out the window, straining to locate the source of the sound, and as I did I realized it wasn't a scream after all—the loud ululation was too controlled to be a howl of anguish or desperation. In the shadows on the opposite side of the concrete pylons that supported the freeway above, I saw what I thought was a bicycle rider and realized that she—from the pitch of the voice it had to be a woman—was singing.

I made a U-turn at Harrison near the leather bar called The Eagle and drove up behind her, catching the bike rider in my headlights. She kept pedaling with her back to me but I recognized Frieda, a full-bodied lady on a three-speed singing an aria in an otherwise deserted city bleakscape, and thought of Fellini as I slid up beside her and, leaning out of my open window, asked, "You take requests?"

Smiling so that I again noticed the passion-gap in her front teeth, she answered, "Sorry, mister, I don't know 'I Left My Dough in San Francisco,' " and then roared with laughter that ricocheted around Division Street. "Hey, big guy, where you been hidin'?" She stopped and straddled her bicycle.

I pulled into the curb ahead of her and got out and walked back. The blinking hazard lights of my taxi cast a pulsating yellow strobe on the empty street. An unseen river of cars whirred past above us, making a sound like the sea.

"Did you hear a driver killed some guy tonight who was trying to rob him?" she asked. "A Metro driver. And if you tell me you were there for this one, too, darlin', then all I'll ask is time to make out my last will and testament before you have your evil way with me."

"It's wonderful to be trusted. You know, your boy Geronimo told me earlier tonight he thought I was a spy."

"Oh, don't mind John, Henry; he can be hotheaded but he's true blue."

"True blue to what?"

"To getting us a fair shake, the Alliance."

"It's been a long time since I believed political correctness was a test of character, Frieda. Geronimo's a brat."

"Whatever," she said.

"Actually, I *was* over there where the Metro driver shot that guy. I heard the thing being called on the police scanner." I told her what I had seen and heard. I could see it disturbed her, so I put my hand on her shoulder and gave a quick squeeze. She leaned momentarily against me and I was surprised that my body responded in a vaguely sexual way. Jessica, damn, when are you coming back? Frieda and I danced one of those awkward little fandangos that I thought would end with adolescence, but hadn't; I pulled away, and we both pretended not to have noticed the complex exchange that had taken place.

"I've been looking for you," I said. "I had a talk with Wiley Nottingham. He says the Police Commission won't go for the three hundred medallions and he thinks some kind of compromise can be worked out. He's not really as much of a slickster as I thought, you know. I think there's more to him than just his gorgeous suits and billboard looks."

Frieda reacted sharply. "Don't be naive. That man . . ." I

think she must have read the surprise on my face, because she pulled up short. "Never mind, darlin', you're probably right. I was just thinking, you know, about what we talked about the morning of the demo. What was it somebody said about the only constant being change? I was thinking about how there was a time when I was one hundred percent certain I knew what was wrong, and then there was even a time when I was pretty sure I knew what was right, and now . . . I used to say to myself that whatever comes down I can live with it. But I chickened out on myself, you know?" She was supporting her bike with one hand and rubbing her upper arm with the other.

I was only half listening because somebody was approaching us along the sidewalk and I was watching their progress, trying to decide whether there was any cause for alarm, as there so easily could be in that place at that time of night. "And now?" I said to Frieda, making out the stooped figure of a bag lady with her worldly possessions in a grocery cart.

"I'm frightened, darlin'. Good and goddamn scared."

"Well, if Edwards was the one, it won't be scary anymore," I said, trying to be reassuring while thoughts of the way the dead man's head had looked troubled my mind and heart. "You'll be okay, you know what you're doing out there."

"So did Pachter and Al Dwiri, that's the thing," she said. "You can't ever be sure what's coming at you or where from, that's the thing. You see?" There was an intensity of feeling in what she was saying, as if she wanted me to see past the words to the secret feelings behind them.

"Anyway," I said, "you were great with Abigail."

"Yeah, darlin', I've always been great." It sounded like a lament.

"I didn't tell you before, but when we were down at City Hall I did a little checking and found out some stuff that may help. Before this last election the taxi companies made just token contributions to Miz Goodman, the obligatory hundred bucks, that kind of thing. What they give to every candidate. But beginning this January all of them dug deeper for the Friends of Abigail Committee. Checker, Frisco, Metro, even the Chinaman's company, a grand, fifteen hundred bucks apiece. Total of about seventy-five hundred.''

Frieda whistled through the gap in her teeth. "So there's more to the new medallions than just Sally Bender getting her boopie wet.''

"It surely looks that way. Abigail's committee's taken in something like eighty thousand in the past few months and there's no local election this year. It's a war chest, and I would guess it's so she can campaign for Vice President, for the nomination. Entertainment, maybe some grease. She must be cutting deals all over town. The taxi companies are just a part of something bigger as far as she's concerned. But she got the message to them that if they supported a local daughter's efforts to make history, she could certainly understand how necessary it was to get some new medallions in their hands. Sally Bender's unfortunate experience was just the excuse she needed.''

"You know, that's really dynamite,'' Frieda said. "I mean, she's supposed to be so clean you can eat off her, right?'' She gave her big laugh, the one that began in her trained diaphragm. "You're coming to the Police Commission hearing, right? Maybe we can embarrass them a little with that stuff.''

"And Nottingham told me that whatever Lemon and the companies are telling you, behind the scenes they're pushing for the medallions the way you thought. Listen, Frieda, why don't you throw your bike in the trunk and I'll run you home before I turn the cab in.''

"No, thanks, darlin'. It's a nice offer but I like to ride along and sing this time of night. It's the way I get my important thinking done.''

"I think it's dangerous,'' I said, surprising myself with my avuncular concern.

"Hey! My singin' ain't *that* bad."

I laughed. She climbed back on her bike. "You know, Henry, you don't believe it, but I think our time's gónna come."

"What were you singing?" I asked diplomatically.

"It's the recognition scene from *Elektra*," she said. "You know it?"

I shook my head no.

"Orest!" she sang, the name reverberating. "Orest!" The cry of her song echoed through the night as she pedaled away, waving goodbye.

I felt melancholy but didn't understand why I should. Maybe it was because there is no greater sorrow than two people with love to give, but not to each other.

Thirteen

The rabbi took a sugar cube from a ceramic bowl on his desk and popped it into his mouth, where it made a bulge in his cheek. He picked up the glass of hot tea gingerly with soft fingertips, blew on it, and took a dainty sip before he placed it back on a round white coaster with a picture of a pale blue dove grasping an olive branch in its beak.

"My grandma drank it that way," I said. "She said it was the old-country way."

"You're an Ashkenazi?" the rabbi asked. "Your family is from Russia?"

"My father's family, from Kerchinov, yes."

"It was a great city. But the pogroms were very bad." He leaned back in his chair and sighed. His tie knot was pulled off center, half under his collar. Making a pyramid with his fingers, he said, "This madman, you think he may be a Jew, then?"

The thought distressed him. He had round smooth cheeks with a pink flush under the dense, close-shaven beard, thick red lips, and doleful eyes behind his glasses. He was about forty and had a well-fed, well-scrubbed look. He appeared to be both young and old, you could see he had changed very little since he had been bar mitzvahed, and I guessed that even at thirteen there had been a grown-upness about him. A born mensch. It was hard to imagine him ever having a carefree childhood.

His office in the modern brick-and-glass synagogue was lined with crammed bookshelves, and papers covered every inch of available surface. There was a shofar, a ceremonial ram's horn, hanging on the wall behind him. The curtains were drawn against the daylight, and the room was lit by a high-wattage overhead light.

"Not necessarily. Knowing one word of Hebrew doesn't a Jew make."

He nodded his agreement. "There have been very few Jewish murderers, thank God. I have heard many explanations for why this should be, but the one I have never heard is, I think, closer to the truth than all the rest. The *Kashrut*." From the way he smiled I knew what he had said was clever. He must have seen that his witticism was lost on me. "The dietary laws," he explained. "You see, only the *shochet*, the ritual butcher, can slaughter an animal in accordance with the *Kashrut*. Consider, then, that no Jewish mother ever killed a chicken with her own hands, and maybe you will have an explanation for why Jews are not murderers. But I am wasting your valuable time. What you want from me is to do with *emet*, truth, the Seal of the Holy One. You have maybe heard of Rabbi Loew of Prague?"

"No. You had better assume I know nothing, Rabbi Hersch. My family wasn't observant; in fact my mother wasn't Jewish. My father's father, when he was a boy, chalked on the wall of the Hillel, 'If every year we say "next year in Jerusalem," doesn't that mean we don't expect ever to get there?' "

"A skeptic. Rabbi Loew had a bit of the skeptic in him, you know—all scientists do, I think—and he was a great scientist, an alchemist, and a cabalist. A true man of his time, of the Renaissance. He wrote prolifically, you know, but never once a word about the golem. Yet the legend is usually attributed to him. Who knows how these things happen?"

"And Rabbi Loew and the legend of the golem, you think this has something to do with the killer writing *emet* in blood near the bodies of his victims?"

"Here, let me show you." He took a fountain pen, and turning a writing tablet halfway around so it was between us, he wrote three Hebrew characters, the same ones I had seen in Greg White's cab. "Aleph Mem Tof, like so," he said. "Now take away the Aleph." He drew a line through it. "What you have left is *met*. 'Death.'

"The word 'golem' appears only once in the Bible, in Genesis. It describes Adam when he was flesh but not yet a man. He had vitality, but not *ru'ah*—spirit, *neshamah*—soul, or *nefesh*—life.

"In the late seventeenth century the legend began to grow that the Jews of Prague had fashioned a great clay idol to defend them. It was said that across its forehead they wrote *emet*, and it awoke from its sleep of clay and became a thing with vitality, a golem. In some early discussions it was said that the act of creation, for want of a better way of putting it, involved making the idol from virgin soil, then walking in a circle around it chanting Aleph Mem Tof and the name of Yahweh. To reduce it to clay again, to dust, you rub out the Aleph and walk around it in the opposite direction. According to Rabbi Ben Sidra, the golem itself was supposed to have given a warning against idol worship and demanded its own destruction after it had served its purpose by defending the Jews of Prague against their persecutors."

"It sounds like the first Frankenstein's monster," I said.

"Yes, but the purpose was good, to create a savior. Maybe the mistake was that man should not try to fabricate himself, or else what he has invented will turn on him and destroy him."

"Bad news for the California ethos."

"Change is, I think, not to be valued for its own sake. God's gift of life is best celebrated humbly."

The telephone rang. It was answered elsewhere in the synagogue, and then a red light glowed on the rabbi's telephone. He pushed a button and asked, "Who is it, Gladys? Ah. Tell Mr. Birnbaum I've got it all arranged and that I'll call him back. And take any messages, will you.

"I'm sorry for the interruption," he told me. "You will forgive the pun, Mr. Henry, but sometime in the seventeenth century the legend of the golem began to take on a life of its own. We have records of learned men in heated discussion about whether a golem can be included to make up a *minyan*, the ten men you need to hold services. In some writings the golem began to be related to tales of the resurrection of the dead."

"It makes me wonder, Rabbi, if the killer might not be a 'dead man,' somebody who died for an instant and was brought back to life. Or a survivor of a suicide attempt."

The rabbi shrugged his rounded shoulders. "I leave the detective work to you and the police, although I doubt it myself, unless your killer has made a study of some obscure eighteenth-century texts which exist only in the original Hebrew as far as I know. Maybe more to the point, in nineteenth-century Germany the Jews had to defend themselves against ritual murder accusations after there had been a number of unexplained murders and somebody all of a sudden remembered about these clay Frankensteins the Jews were said to create with their own black magic. Could this not happen again? It is very sad the way ignorance and fear seek scapegoats. Not so different, either, from the way certain people in our own time say AIDS is God's will. I don't know, excuse me for rambling afield. Does any of this really help you?"

"Maybe, I'm not really sure. The police don't seem to have much to go on. What you're telling me fits a possible profile of a psychopath, a man completely lacking moral sense, a golem of sorts. A man who is asking to be found and destroyed. How difficult is it to learn about Rabbi Loew and his legend?"

"It comes up from time to time in books about the occult, and I have come across it in scholarly works about Mary Shelley. There were even two films that I know of, a silent German work and then a French remake. As for yourself, if you want to know more I would suggest a very interesting

novel by Gustav Meyrink called *Der Golem*. It's been translated into English. A terrifying book, an allegory about man's
reduction to an automaton by the pressures of modern living.
I'm sorry, but I really don't see what more help I can be."
He popped another sugar cube, and took a long swallow from
his glass of tea. "God forbid he's a Jew."

"I appreciate your help." I stood and so did he.

"Maybe we'll see you again under more pleasant circumstances. The Succoth festival is soon. You would enjoy it
even if your grandfather wouldn't have."

I laughed and headed for the door.

"There is a statue of him, you know, Mr. Henry, at the
entrance to the Town Hall in Prague."

For a moment I wasn't sure whom he meant. "Of Rabbi
Loew?"

"Jehuda Loew ben Bezalel, yes. Who else? Of course, it is
not the man himself. Just his likeness in clay."

Fourteen

If I hadn't promised Frieda that I would be there, wild horses could not have dragged me to the Police Commission meeting. The auditorium was packed, but the commissioners were too busy deciding what to do when they did arrive in public to actually show up on time.

Back in the far corner of the auditorium a driver began to stamp his feet with impatience. His cadence was taken up by somebody else, and then other feet began the ponderous tattoo, until the entire room rocked to the beat of the heavy thumping. My legs remained crossed, I could never participate in mass clapping—not even at a ball game—without feeling like a Nazi.

"Strike! Strike! Strike! Strike!" They chanted in cadence with their beating feet. The commission was an hour late. "Executive session" was the sanitizing expression for what they were up to, and there was a law against it, a law none of the four uniforms positioned around the jammed auditorium seemed inclined to enforce.

Not that the SFPD was asleep on the job, far from it. Geronimo lit a cigarette and immediately one of the cops padded up. "There's no smoking allowed," he said.

Geronimo turned on him, the tendons in his neck taut and his face red. For an awful moment I thought he was going to swing on the cop. But he stubbed the cigarette out under his heel. The cop hesitated as if making up his mind whether to make an issue of that, but then straightened up and resumed his post at the side of the room.

Finally a door opened behind the long, raised podium occupied only by five empty swivel chairs with nameplates and microphones in front of them, and the members of the commission came in single file and took their seats. The stomping and chanting faltered, picked up and became strident again, and then petered out.

The chairman, a middle-aged Mexican insurance broker named Lopez, tapped his microphone with a pencil to see if it was live, and the sharply amplified tapping caused a wave of nervous titters. Lopez was flanked by a sideshow display of the circus that was San Francisco politics. To his left sat a Chinese real estate agent and a lesbian consultant. To his right was a black college administrator whose uncle ran the numbers racket in Bayview-Hunter's Point, and a retired police chief. Each and every one of them was wholly beholden to Abigail Goodman for his political life, but who was counting?

"Ladies and gentlemen," said Lopez, whose interest in police work was said to have flourished with the wife of the captain of detectives, "we must have order for conducting this meeting of the Police Commission of the City and County of San Francisco." They loved the phrase "City and County of San Francisco": it made them feel important to have their lips around it.

I turned in my seat to look at the wall clock and saw that Dropo, Big John Lemon, and Wiley Nottingham had just come into the auditorium and were standing together at the back. It was apparent that they had been closeted with the commissioners in executive session. I nudged Frieda and motioned toward them. She turned and had a look. When she caught Dropo's eyes she waved gaily.

To me she said, "See no evil, hear no evil, speak no evil. Madam Mayor's a monkey grinder."

"You have to admit it's sporting of her not to make them wear their collars in public."

"She's got their family jewels in her office safe, darlin'. If they misbehave she won't give 'em back."

Lopez called on Nottingham to speak for the mayor, whose presence, he said, was regrettably required elsewhere, and Wiley prowled forward in an elegantly cut and draped three-piece suit with double vents. I knew about the vents in the gray herringbone because a lectern had been placed facing the board, so Wiley stood with his back to us.

Nottingham talked in the argot of bureaucrats about why the mayor believed three hundred new taxis were urgently required, referring to occupancy ratios, permit distribution phase-ins, administrative oversight, registration functions, and other ripe pickings from the tree of political knowledge that in their way were no less arcane than Teenage Mutant Ninja Turtles.

He was still nattering when a driver stood and shouted, "How'd you like it if we doubled the people doing your job and split the salary?" Shouts and clapping rippled across the room.

"Order!" Lopez said loudly. "Order! Everybody who wants to speak will be heard."

"Everyone you listen to has been heard already!" came an answering shout.

"Railroad!"

Things continued like that. The only surprise was a driver who approached the lectern slowly with a pronounced limp and stood patiently until he had an attentive silence. Then very distinctly he said, "We have families to support, sir," turned, and made his way back to his seat.

A while later the retired police chief made a motion that almost nobody in the room heard, Lopez called for a show of hands, all five went up displaying their variety of skin shades, and before anybody knew exactly what had happened the board rose and filed out. One of the cops stationed himself in front of the door through which they had exited with his hands folded across his chest.

"What the hell happened?" Geronimo asked Frieda, a

question being repeated throughout the room. I got up and went over to Sue Yeh, a *Courier* reporter who had been sitting in the front row taking notes. She said they had approved one hundred fifty new medallions immediately, with the others to be phased in in stages, and I brought that information back to Frieda.

A lot of angry drivers were heading over to a bar on 16th Street to plan their next step and Frieda asked if I was coming, too, but I figured I could live without the hours of bitching and posturing I knew would be the main order of business. I told her I would call her so we could talk it over. On my way out I overheard a driver saying in an anguished voice, "They never even mentioned the guys who were killed. Frank Iancini was a partner of mine. You think those cocksuckers care if we live or die?"

Emet, the whole *emet,* and nothing but the *emet.*

When I pulled into my private parking spot in the alley behind the bookstore, North Beach was bustling with people made restless by an unseasonable patch of fine summer weather. I was antsy, too, and hesitated about what to do before I trudged upstairs to my solitary but immaculate abode. I switched on a standing lamp and paced aimlessly from room to room.

There were plenty of numbers in my little book that I could call, and even a few I didn't have to look up in the book or hesitate about calling at this late hour. Jessica and I had known each other a short time, but since we had become lovers I hadn't called any of the other numbers. Nothing was stopping me except the way I knew I would feel afterward if I did call. At times in the past that hadn't been enough to tame boredom, lust, loneliness, masochism, and the other elements that comprised temptation.

I was relieved when there was no answer at Erica's phone. More than relieved. I felt saved. Some nights a lonely bed feels better than you expect.

Fifteen

I was cleaning and oiling the Walther while the Giants were being creamed by the Braves on the radio. It was hot and muggy in Atlanta and the Giants were suffering. In San Francisco a wispy fog was cooling the memory of a rare hot day. My only plan was to finish with the gun and then, when the Braves were finished with the Giants, to cross Columbus to Tosca's and do what I could to get well oiled myself.

For a couple of days life had been feeling like one of those dreams where you're trying to get somewhere but are forever being diverted so that the frustration and the urgency make you frantic. It meant some impulse deep in my subconscious was making its sluggish way toward consciousness. Outside on Columbus people were out having fun. Who were my fellow city dwellers, where had they all come from, these people whose shadows were not dogged by The Shadow? Where had the Prophet of Doom come from, and how had he mutated?

He used a knife to kill, a very sharp knife. That seemed important. But why? It had been more than three weeks since Greg White had become his fourth victim on the same night that Jessica had flown home to England. Since then not a peep out of either of them. I had fought the urge to call her and she had not been in touch with me. My interpretation of what her silence meant was as steadfast as Hamlet's resolve.

Knowing that the killer seemed to be aware of the legend of the golem might have helped me to understand his thinking, but it hadn't brought me any closer to finding him. In San Francisco even murder was a source of fun and even Gino, who wore grease-stained aprons over his beer belly and shaved only on alternate Tuesdays, participated in the joke. That morning he had asked me what you call a homicidal maniac with a machete in his hand. Sir!

The Prophet might have gone to ground, or left the city altogether, or even been in jail on some unrelated charge. That sort of thing happened. The Zodiac killer had disappeared and nobody had ever known who he had been or what had become of him. Maybe he was running a nursery school or had found work as an astrologer to the stars. I sensed from the heavy feeling of muted frustration that pervaded my thinking that I was missing the obvious, that between the golem and the razor's edge fell some shadow I should be able to see but just could not.

I picked up the telephone on the third ring. I never answered on the first ring, and when I was lonely not even on the second so as not to tip an empty hand.

"Yep?" I cradled the phone between my neck and my shoulder so I could keep wiping down the Walther.

"You sound as if you're pretending to be American." The connection was perfectly clear, too clear, I hoped, to be international.

"No, I'm the real McCoy." On the other hand, if she had been back for awhile and not called, that was bad.

"McCoy was a Scotsman," she said. "You sound so American I can't believe you're serious."

"I think it's just that your ears have become British again. You need aural reorientation therapy."

"It's a good idea, that. Will you help me?"

"Yes."

"Will you come fetch me from in front of the international terminal?"

"Yes."

I heard the receiver being replaced.

I left the gun beside the telephone and concentrated the entire way to the airport on restraining my foot from punishing the gas pedal. It seemed important to drive no faster than usual.

She was waiting. As we embraced I inhaled the half-forgotten scent of her, and my hands traced the ridges of muscle down her back. "You sounded so American, for a moment I felt I didn't know you at all. I thought it was all a mistake. Is it?"

"No, it isn't," I said, with a solemnity that surprised me. I opened the car door. As she arranged herself on the seat her skirt slid up her thighs.

Her smile was knowing. "Come on, then, don't just moon around as if we have all night."

"Don't we?"

"We'll always be in a rush. If we're ever not in a rush, that will be death for us. That's just the way it is. Neither of us knows a thing about being steadfast, Hank. What we know is how fast we run together."

As I started out into traffic Jessica said, "I tell you what I want. I want a doughnut. I want a whole bag full of doughnuts."

I put my hand on her inner thigh. "I know a place," I said.

She slid closer to me and breathed warmly against my ear. "You have awfully big ears."

She closed her legs and trapped my hand tight between her thighs. "What was the first thing you noticed about me?"

"That first time I saw you in the bookstore? The way your bracelets slithered down your long, slim wrist."

"Like this?"

I reached for her.

"Keep your eyes on the road, laddie. I didn't defy the laws of gravity for twelve hours to get squashed like a bug in an oversize American car driving on the wrong side of the road because you can't keep your mind on what you're doing.''

I had to clear my throat before I could ask, ''Your husband?''

''That's all been taken care of,'' she said.

''What did you tell him? About us.''

''Everything that was necessary.''

''Everything?'' I was thrown by that. I moved my hand on her thigh.

''Of course not,'' she said, removing my hand. ''Michael is my best friend.''

It made me feel as if I had been delivered into his hands, and I didn't much like it. ''What did he say?''

''He was badly hurt, but he never talks about what he's feeling. He said he wanted me to be happy.''

''He wasn't angry? What's wrong with him?''

''Unlike you and me, he loves unselfishly. It's something I don't think you can really understand.'' She looked away from me.

''I'm sorry, I've missed you. I've been lonely and it's a feeling I hate, I'm used to being alone. I've had to stop my imagination from doing its usual dirty work. And I feel like there's something about the Prophet of Doom I should be understanding but just can't.''

''The Prophet of Doom?''

''That's what they're calling the taxi killer. I'll tell you all about it. But later.''

''Michael wanted me to stay with him,'' she said. ''I told him I couldn't. He understood. It made him very sad and I felt awful about it. I think it's worse to be the one who leaves than the one who is left.''

''I would never let you walk away from me without a fight.''

''Do you mean that? It frightens me.''

''I would come after you,'' I said. ''Doesn't that please you, too?''

''Yes, I'm pleased you feel that strongly about me. But it

frightens me to think you would try to prevent me from doing what I wanted.''

"Tell me more about him," I said.

"We met at university, when I was eighteen. He comes from a very good family. They're brokers in the City. His name is Michael Gage. When we met he was studying medicine. His father wanted him to join the family firm but he hated finance. For a year or two I thought I was in love with him, and by the time that wore off we were married. He's an awfully nice man and I'm very, very fond of him. But the marriage didn't take at all: we became friends. He's very self-contained and it drives me mad. English men drive me mad; my lovers have all been foreign. I don't stay in one place for very long. So if you expect too much from me you'll only be disappointed. I can't rely on myself. You shouldn't rely on me either.

"Michael has heard stories from me about other men in the past. He expects he knows the ending."

"This is not the same. I am not other men."

"No. And I am here with you. And want my doughnuts."

As I waited for her at the curb, jealousy, desire, hope caution, pride, and disbelief all had their say. She came back to the car from the twenty-four-hour doughnut shop carrying a white bag and two coffees in containers. She handed me mine and we both rested them on the dashboard. Circles of warm moisture formed on the windshield above them. She unfolded the white sack and peered inside. Her fingers were long and supple, slim with no fleshy padding, da Vinci rather than Botticelli hands. I imagined them at seventy with swollen joints. They would still be beautiful. I imagined them pressed palms down against my chest and shivered.

She turned to look at me then, her green eyes narrowed, and held the sack of doughnuts toward me. I shook my head no. She reached into the sack and chose a chocolate glazed cruller. She put it down beside her coffee. She said, "I love you."

It was as if a grenade had detonated against my rib cage. From where I had slumped against the car door I searched for the right words. What came out wasn't original but it was true, that single sentence free of falsehood whose existence I had doubted just a few weeks ago. "I've been looking for you my whole life," I said.

Sixteen

We were in that nether state between wakefulness and sleep that is pure sensual bliss when the insistent ringing of the phone pried us reluctantly apart. Removing my body from hers, even for an instant, seemed a criminal shame. But when Peter didn't answer, as he had answered earlier calls since we had come back to my place, I realized it was past one a.m. and the service was closed for the night.

"I don't want to get out of bed," I said. "I'm not going to answer it."

Her face was close to mine on the pillow, her eyes dreamy and amused. Strands of black hair had fallen over her wide mouth. She blew them away. "It's some hussy you took up with while I was in England, isn't it?" Jessica threw back the sheet and walked to the telephone. I watched her with a deep gratitude.

Whoever was on the other end paused before speaking when they heard her voice. When the caller finally spoke I could hear it was a woman but not what she was saying. As Jessica listened she glared at me with her head cocked to one side.

"No," she said. "Who may I say called?" Frosty and formal. She listened for another moment and then put the receiver back on its cradle. She picked up the Walther from where I had left it when I went to the airport.

"I've never held a gun before," she said. "It's awfully heavy, isn't it? Are there bullets in it?"

"No. It takes a clip and there's none in it, but don't touch the trigger or that little catch. You can't be too careful."

"Why do you have it out?"

"I was cleaning it."

"It's a ghastly thing." She put it back down on the desk. "Is it something to do with the Prophet of Doom? God, that's so apocalyptic." She wrapped her arms around her chest but stayed where she was, not returning to bed.

"Oiling it is just something that has to be done. He killed another one, it was the night you left. And a taxi driver shot some guy who was a suspect and might have been trying to rob him. The killer's still out there."

I told Jessica about Aleph Mem Tof and the legend of the golem. When I finished I said, "Come back to bed."

Instead she reached over and took my shirt off the back of the desk chair, slipping into it and buttoning one button. "Who is Frieda and why is it so important for her to talk with you at this time of night?"

Damn! I had forgotten to call Frieda the way I had said I would after the Police Commission meeting. Well, it could wait until the morning. "She's the leader of the Alliance. I was supposed to call her. I've gotten to know her a lot better since you've been gone. She's brave to be doing what she's doing, standing up to the company. And when the mayor was giving the drivers a lot of shit and then rubbing their noses in it, Frieda made a really fine gesture," I said, thinking of the umbrella. "If the drivers have any chance of not being completely crushed, it's only because of her."

"Is she very pretty?"

"Frieda? She once was, but now she must weigh two hundred pounds and she's a couple of inches shorter than you."

"You're comparing her to me? I suppose I come out wanting."

"Jessica, come back to bed with me."

"You fancy her."

"That's ridiculous. C'mon over here and old Hank'll show you who he likes to hanky-pank with."

"I don't know if I believe you," she said, but she came back to the bed. In a moment, though, she popped up again.

"I've never known anybody as restless as you are," I said.

"What about you?"

We laughed.

"She likes *you*."

"I don't know. Not really. I mean, how would I know?"

"Just listen to you. Of course she likes you. Wipe that smile off your face, Hank, or you'll regret it. She's obsessed with you, why else would she be ringing you in the middle of the night?"

"She's not obsessed with me. And it's not so late for a night-shift driver." All I cared about at the moment was getting Jessica back into my bed.

She was looking at a photograph I had hung above my desk. "Who are the fighters? Is it Muhammad Ali?"

"No, it's Jersey Joe Walcott getting knocked out by Rocky Marciano. The first fight. The fight was a long time ago, in the early fifties. It's the first thing I can ever remember seeing on television. Marciano, he's the white guy, he was very hard, he won forty-nine fights without ever losing one. He was a fighter of brute force. Walcott was years older, he was the champion, but Marciano wore Joe down and knocked him out in thirteen. Jersey Joe had fought with so much heart they gave him a second shot.

"He was being offered his last chance at a big payday. All he had to do for it was take one more beating from a younger man he knew he could never, ever beat. He had nothing to prove, not to himself, not to anyone. He got the second fight over with as fast as he could. The first time Marciano hit him hard he went down and stayed down."

While I was telling her about Jersey Joe, Jessica had

returned to the bed beside me. "You find losing more interesting than winning, don't you?"

"I suppose I do. Winning always seems to me like the same story. But there are an infinite number of sorrows in what we can lose. And an infinite number of chances to salvage something important to us. I don't know, maybe that's just sentimentality. Maybe the second fight was fixed, maybe Jersey Joe was paid to go into the tank in the first round."

"Aren't you going to call your Frieda?"

"It can wait."

"I'll be glad when this Prophet of Doom is found," she said. Then she touched me in a way that made me gasp with surprise and pleasure.

Seventeen

A few white cottony clouds breezed through an otherwise blue morning sky. The day promised to be another tourist bureau promissory note honored by the Big Shill in the sky. From the Golden Gate you saw an enchanted city dolled up in its finery and its jewels like a beautiful woman at a fancy ball. I prefer the view from the Bay Bridge of the same woman, her makeup erased by the sheets, in her nightgown, her hair tousled, drinking a cup of coffee in an open window after a night of love.

At the last minute I decided not to take the North Beach exit and instead continued toward the central freeway. I had dropped Jessica early at her place in the Berkeley hills. I was ravenously hungry and on the spur of the moment I headed toward the Haight to buy Frieda a breakfast that would make amends for my not having called her when I said I would.

I was bursting with bonhomie and took pleasure in the thought of what I could do to please. Jewish girls were the best girls to eat with, and fat Jewish girls were sublime at table. There was a place a block from Frieda's flat that put on a good feed in the morning. It served only whole grain toast, but a man in love is prepared to forgive such wholesome sins.

I crossed the Panhandle and turned onto Frieda's street. What I saw changed my mood as swiftly and categorically as a Dear John letter. I took in the scene one piece at a time.

First, commotion and confusion. Then, the black-and-whites. Then, Browder and Corelli. They were standing beside Checker 509. Oh, no, I thought, please, no, make it all a mistake.

When I reached them Corelli was stubbing out a cigarette with his heel.

"Is she dead?" I asked.

"What, are we here for our health? Jimmy, Henry here thinks Homicide is coming out to scenes for the fresh air."

"Same M.O.?" I asked Browder, who replied by opening the door to the taxi. They had already taken Frieda away, but there on the windshield was the familiar message: Aleph Mem Tof. *Emet,* truth. And death. This time, though, there was a second message, in what looked like lipstick, smeared across the tan seat in shaky letters, like a child's painting: N O. And a squiggly dash that looked as if it had been made as her hand faltered and fell.

The sour, meaty smell of coagulating blood mixed with the stale odor of the cab and a third smell that somehow was inappropriate, a sweet vegetative smell that was there and then gone, tantalizing and elusive. I backed out of the taxi.

"NO?"

Browder shrugged. "Looks like."

"You shut off the meter?" I asked Browder.

"Nah. I suppose the first uniform did it, I don't know."

"When was it reported?"

"Hour and a half ago. A neighbor called in to complain because the cab was stopped across her driveway. She hadn't heard or seen anything. I got people doing door-to-door now but we won't get much until tonight, a lot of people are at work."

"Can you beat that?" Corelli said. "Did you know there was anybody in the Haight Ashbury who worked?"

"She lived right over there," Browder said. "Frieda Mishkin."

"Yeah, I know. Any idea when she was killed?"

"Klein says between midnight and four is his preliminary

guess. I'll have a report after lunch sometime. Sharp blade along the throat again, same perpetrator.''

Corelli started needling me again. ''We're dillying our dallies out here because the mayor's going to make the chief's hemorrhoids ache and he's going to clean the lieutenant's eardrums and guess who the lieutenant's going to tell bedtime stories to. You think the Democrats are really dumb enough to make her Vice President? Let the cops run the department again? I got to be dreaming, right? Jimmy, let's get our wives to light candles for her.''

I wasn't paying much attention to Corelli because I was squirming to wriggle free of my guilty conscience. How big a deal would it have been to talk to Frieda when she had called last night and said it was important? Was that all she had said? I wanted to get to a phone and call Jessica and ask her. ''I don't ever want to get out of bed''—was that what I had said when the phone rang? And then we had flirted, made a flirtation out of whatever fear or distress had made Frieda call at midnight or later, only hours or even minutes before she was murdered. I had been so absorbed in getting Jessica back beside me that I hadn't even acknowledged to myself that it was late for a phone call. I hadn't thought about anything except my own pleasure, me the wise guy who had all those put-downs at the tip of his tongue when it came to people who liked to have fun. Oh, yeah, I was quite a guy. A hell of a guy. Poor Frieda, to have nobody better than me to call upon when she was in trouble.

''She was a friend of yours, this Mishkin?'' Browder said, reading my face.

''Sort of.'' I didn't want to say anything about the phone call until I talked with Jessica. ''Can I come by later when you've got Klein's report and . . . you know, later?''

''Sure, sure. We got to get back now anyway. Henry?''

''Yeah?''

''I played ball with you on this thing for no good reason. You understand? They ain't going to be pinning no diapers on any duck's ass about this, you know what I mean? I'm sorry about your friend, but what you got, I need.''

"Hey, Jimmy, you forget what a smart boy Henry is, or what? He knows what you're telling him. You don't have to mention him withholding evidence or nothing for him to catch on. He's right with it.''

"You know something, Corelli?' I said. "Your mother raised an asshole.''

He had been chewing a toothpick and now he spat it out and stepped toward me. I balled my fists, aching to smash his smirking face.

"Shit.'' Browder turned and started back toward their unmarked car in his splay-footed walk. Corelli hesitated, then grinned and went after him.

I was on my way back to my own car when an old red Volkswagen beetle came hurtling around the corner without even slowing down for the light and slammed to a stop beside me. I wasn't prepared for what happened next.

Geronimo was on top of me before I had time to react. A long, looping right hand caught me high on the cheekbone and staggered me. Both his big hands seized hold of my collar as he tried to get a grip on my throat. Instinctively I drove a knee hard into his groin. He let go of my throat and doubled over with his hands between his legs. I moved to my left to get a better angle and was about to bludgeon him across the back of the neck when I caught myself and dropped my fist. I helped him down onto the pavement, although he twisted away and spat toward me. It was all I could do not to kick him in the face.

"What the hell is the matter with you?''

"You egotistical bastard, I'm going to kill you. You hear me?'' The words came out in gasps, squeezed by pain.

"What is it, Geronimo? Why me?''

"You're too fucking full of yourself to even know she was stuck on you, aren't you, you prick? She was just a fat girl to you. Oh, man,'' he said, more to himself than to me, "I loved her.'' He sobbed.

I half turned away and waited for him to gain control of himself. When he had quieted down and hauled himself to his feet, still bent over from the waist, I said, "I'm sorry. I really am. I didn't know about any of that." My right cheek just below the eye was starting to hurt and I could feel it swelling.

"You're going to wish you never met me."

"I do already. Did you see her last night? I think she knew something was wrong, that she was in some kind of trouble. Do you know anything about that?"

"There was a steering committee meeting but she phoned up and said she couldn't make it, she had something to do that couldn't wait. I came around here after and rang her bell, but she wasn't home. She wasn't with you?"

"With me? Whatever gave you that idea?"

"You're an unfeeling bastard, you know that? She talked about you all the time. Ben says this, Ben says we should do that."

"I had no idea."

"But you think you know every fucking thing there is to know. Well, fuck you." He limped back to his car.

Back at my place, I called Jessica's house but there was no answer. So I dialed the service.

"Oh, Be-en," Peter said. "Where were you last night? That poor woman wanted to talk so bad."

"Frieda Mishkin?" I asked with a sinking heart.

"Yes, Ben. You know, then? She has reached you? She called at eleven, and then she called at twelve. I didn't know what to tell her."

"Did she say what it was about?"

"Only that it was *very* important you heard her message. But I could feel something was wrong. I could feel the vibes, Ben."

"Listen, Peter, if Jessica calls tell her I must talk to her as soon as possible. Tell her I'll be trying her, but she should try me, too. Would you?"

"Oh, Jessica's back? When did she return to us, Ben? It will be good to hear her voice."

"You'll give her my message?"

"Of course, Ben. If she calls. Ciao."

By the time I reached the Hall of Justice the bruise on my cheek where Geronimo had hit me had turned into an angry red lump. Browder and Corelli were at their desks, which were pushed together facing each other. Corelli gave me a look that would have scared the eggs out of a hen.

"Anything?" I asked Browder, sitting down. His jacket was off and his revolver was hanging beneath his left arm in a worn leather holster.

"That was what I asked you," he said. Corelli wanted to grin, but it came out a grimace limned by malicious glee.

"She was trying to reach me last night. Called twice, at eleven and twelve, but I wasn't there. My service took the messages. It sounded like something was wrong with her." As soon as the words were out of my mouth I recognized that I shouldn't have told them that the service took the messages; to spare myself I had put Peter in jeopardy. They were sure to want to talk with him, and Peter was in the country illegally, without a green card. Quite a guy, I was quite a guy. The only way I could change my story now would mean it would be Jessica they would question instead. What a goddamn mess I was making.

"Somebody knocked some sense into his head, Jim," Corelli said wickedly. "What's the name of the service?"

"Actually, to tell you the truth, I talked with her myself. I was just trying to save myself the embarrassment. She said there was some trouble, but I was tied up, uh, I was with a friend." A friend. "And, I, you know, I shined her off. I didn't listen to what she had to say. I feel rotten about it. Maybe there was something going on that I could have done something about. I didn't."

Browder didn't believe me. "That's it?"

I nodded.

"Klein's report is supposed to be ready," he said to his partner. "If you're not too busy or anything, you think you could go down there and pick it up?"

They understood each other perfectly. "Don't you two tell any secrets while Corelli's gone," he said. As soon as he was out the door I owned up.

"Thanks. The whole truth is that it was the service that took the messages. At eleven and twelve. But the guy you'll want to talk to, I would count it as a favor if you weren't too interested in his immigration status or anything like that." There was no such thing as a trustworthy cop, but I had no choice.

"Is that what was bothering you? That's the feds' business. We got enough problems all our own."

I gave him Peter's name and address and number of the service. "You'll give me a chance to talk to him first? He's a gentle kind of guy."

Browder turned his palm up over the phone, an invitation. I dialed.

"Peter?"

"No word from our Jessica, Ben. I have not forgotten."

"Okay, listen. There's a policeman, he wants to talk to you about those calls from Frieda Mishkin last night. His name is Browder, Detective Browder."

"Oh, Be-en. Oh, I . . ."

"You don't have to be scared, Peter. He's a very understanding man. He wants to talk only about the phone calls, nothing else interests him. You can trust me, Peter." Could he? Frieda had. "Nothing bad is going to happen, do you understand?"

"Yes, but, Ben, I, they, they can . . ."

"It will not happen that way, Peter. You just tell Detective Browder whatever he wants to know and it'll be okay." Browder spun his finger over his watch and pointed out the window. "He'll be over to talk to you in a while. It will be okay, you have my word."

"I wish you hadn't done this, Be-en. My whole life is making a picture in my eyes."

"Call me after he's gone, Peter. You'll feel better then."

"Yes." He sounded very small. I hung up feeling no bigger than a thimbleful of something unpleasant myself.

"Corelli," I began.

"I told you," Browder said.

"Yeah. Yeah, okay. Jesus."

Corelli ambled in with copies of the coroner's report and put one down in front of Browder. I waited while they both read it, Browder slipping on his wobbly half-frames.

"He's getting careless, our boy," Corelli said without looking up.

Browder grunted and kept reading.

I waited.

"He didn't sharpen his knife this time, the cut was jagged," Browder finally told me. "The other four, the knife's been razor-sharp, no pulls or tears of the flesh. I don't see how the hell that's going to help." He put the coroner's report face down on his desk. "Okay?" It was a dismissal.

I got up. Corelli said, "Who hit you?"

"Lover's quarrel." I started out.

"The tough guy got bopped by a girl, Jimmy, you hear that? By a girl."

I kept walking. Poor Malcolm was probably half starved and bursting at the seams by now.

Eighteen

The phone booth in the lobby of the Hall of Justice had a swastika defacing it. It stared angrily at it while I listened to Jessica's telephone ringing in her empty house. In that instant the significance of the perfectly sharpened knife blade clicked. Naturally there were no phone books in any of the booths in the Hall.

I came outside and looked up and down Bryant Street trying to figure out the closest place where I could look at the Yellow Pages. Lloyd's Bail Bond was directly across the street, and despite Seymour's unhappy fate it was still open for business. Inside I found Mrs. Lloyd occupying her late husband's desk. Frankly she looked rosier of cheek than she had when Seymour was still alive.

She was reluctant, but in the end Seymour's merry widow did let me look at her phone book, standing close by me as if she were afraid I was going to grab it and make a run for the door.

About twenty minutes later I pulled up outside Kaplan's Kosher Meats, the only kosher butcher listed in the city. The shop was in a block-long shopping district in the Sunset on a rise from which you could see the implacable blue-gray ocean merging into a heavy fog bank at the western horizon. It was in the middle of the block wedged between Ray's A-1 Good Neighbor Pharmacy and the Four Happinesses Restaurant.

A bell tinkled when I opened the door and entered the shop. There were no customers. A freckled butcher in a smock with his sleeves rolled up over plump pink forearms was sliding a tray of steaks into the refrigerated display cabinet. He finished what he was doing, wiped his hands on the skirt of his smock, and asked what he could do for me today.

"I'm looking for Mr. Kaplan."

"Morris or Marty?"

"I don't know—either, I suppose."

"Morris retired," he said. His voice was high-pitched, squeaky.

"Marty will do fine."

"He only comes in now on Tuesday and Thursday afternoons, Morris. I think he's bored. A man works his whole life, what's he supposed to do when he's got nothing to do? Watch his arteries get hard? Marty's at the bank. You can wait if you want, he should be back in a sec."

The butcher left me alone in the store and went into the back room. After a few minutes he came back with another tray of meat. "Not here yet, huh?" he said, slid the tray into the case, plumped up the steaks until they were arranged to his satisfaction, and returned to the back room, where the butchering was done.

A white Toyota pickup pulled up at a meter outside and a dark-browed man of about forty, wearing a striped polo shirt, jeans, and Frye boots, came into the store carrying an empty canvas bank bag.

"Marty Kaplan?"

"Yeah?" He didn't smile and seemed as suspicious as Mrs. Lloyd had been. I remembered that I had a shiner, that I hadn't shaved, and that I was not sure how to approach what I wanted.

I told him my name and extended a hand. From his hesitation I realized I shouldn't have, he wasn't a hand shaker.

"I'm an investigator working on a case. Can you spare a minute?"

"What case?" He was wary. The first thing on his mind were his insurance rates.

"It's really a long shot, just a hunch really. I'm looking for a husband who skipped out on his child support payments. Three kids, nice kids. Anyway, I think he's living somewhere in the neighborhood, and like I say, it's a hunch, but he's a cook, an amateur gourmet, and his wife said he was fanatical about sharp knives. They used to fight over her blunting his blades. I just wondered if anybody had been in the last few months to have his knives sharpened." I hoped it didn't sound as preposterous to him as it did to me.

"I don't think he was ever married, you can just tell, you know?" Marty Kaplan said. "Some guys just aren't the marrying kind."

Was I finally doing something right? "I know what you mean. But it may be the same guy. What did he look like?"

"Short guy, stocky, kind of foreign but not colored or anything. He wasn't Jewish, but he said he was interested in the dietary laws. I told him, you know, even if he followed the *shehitah*, the laws for taking an animal's life, meat slaughtered by someone who isn't a *shochet*, I mean he wasn't even a Jew, it would still be *trefah*. He was a funny little guy. He said it didn't matter, he only trusted a kosher butcher to sharpen his knife. Why argue, right?"

"That sounds like it could be him. Does he still have that Charlie Chaplin mustache?"

"Nah, he was clean-shaved."

"What kind of knife was it he wanted you to sharpen?"

"Junk. I told him to get a better knife. It was one of those Swiss things, a Victorinox. Eight inches, a cook's knife."

"His wife said he had Swiss knives. So he's interested in kosher dietary laws now, is he?"

"The second time, a couple of months ago, he asked me a lot of questions, you know, like why Jews only eat meat the blood has been drained out of. I gave him the whole spiel, how the blood of the animal is what carries its instincts and passions. If a human being eats the blood of the animal, he's unclean to carry out the teachings of the Torah. What really interested him the most was the kindness to animals; he said he couldn't stand to think about the suffering of animals. He was real human. You wouldn't think a guy like that would run out on his kids. People are nuts, huh?''

"You can say that again." I was trying to hide my excitement. "So the last time he came in was a couple of months ago, April, May, something like that?"

"No, that was the second time. The last time was just, I don't know—oh, yeah, I do, I can tell you exactly. It was June second. The way I remember is, it was the day my father retired and we closed early, you know. To have a little farewell party, forty-five years in the business. He was still hanging around when we locked up, but I let him stay because I was explaining the rules of the *shochet*. First, the knife edge has to be perfect. Even the smallest notch could tear the flesh, and the animal might suffer."

I nodded. That was what had given me the idea to try a kosher butcher.

Marty Kaplan ticked the points off on a thick, raw-looking finger. Butchers' hands, because they are cold or wet most of the time, come to look as raw as the meat they work with. "Two, you kill the animal without any interruption. Three, the animal has got to be able to see the knife. The cut has got to be just exactly horizontal across the windpipe and gullet. If you're too high you can blunt the knife on the cartilaginous ring, it's ossified. But if you're too low you hit the trachea where it begins to divide, you would slice the muscles, that's very painful for the animal."

My Adam's apple bobbed protectively.

"You know what he asked me? Your guy asked me what if I made a mistake? Who would know? You got to discard the whole animal if you miss, it's no joking matter. He even wanted to learn the benediction, he called it. The only part he could get right was *homane*. Amen. I don't think it's your guy, though."

A fearful disappointment struck me. "Why not?"

"He said he had to come all the way out here from the Mission somewhere on the N line and walk over because he couldn't find a cab. He said he took a lot of cabs because he didn't have a car but you could never find one when you needed one. I remember because he got pretty hot about it. I couldn't see it was such a big deal. So he doesn't live in the neighborhood here. You would think somebody who could afford cabs would be able to support his kids."

"So he hasn't been out to have his knife sharpened since June second?" It was the night of the second when I had found Greg White.

"Nah."

For some reason my guy, as Marty Kaplan called him, hadn't bothered to have his knife sharpened for Frieda. Or maybe he had switched butchers, although there was no other kosher butcher in the city, and the job that had been done wasn't up to standard. Maybe he was doing his own sharpening now, laying low because of the publicity. There were a lot of possibilities. One that especially troubled me was that somebody else might have been Frieda's killer. The unsharpened knife wasn't all that was wrong. If Frieda had had a passenger in her cab, the meter should have been running. And why was she parked not only outside her own flat but across a driveway? It all suggested that she had been in her cab with someone she knew, and perhaps on their way to her place, when she suddenly pulled over.

"And the time before that, Marty, was around April?"

"More or less. It was a long time, maybe a couple of months, after the first time. It surprised me he came back."

"The first time was when, winter?"

"Before New Year's, I think. It doesn't matter, does it?"

It mattered more than I could tell Marty. Albert Dwiri had

been murdered on May 4. Iancini was the week before Christmas. Pachter the second week in February. "Are you sure he didn't come in one other time? Around February?"

"Sure I'm sure. 'Course, I don't know about all of February because we took the kids to Hawaii. Maybe my father would know. I don't see how it makes any difference to his wife and kids if he did or didn't. You want me to ask my father?"

"Would you?"

"Sure, why not." He went off into the back room. I waited, fidgeting. When he returned he said, "Now, how the hell did you know that? I called my father, he says some guy came in asking for me to sharpen his knife. When he told him I was on vacation, the guy asked him to do it instead. He remembers because he charged him two bucks and the guy complained, he said I never charged him. You were right, the bum is a cheapskate, isn't he?"

Nineteen

The Jews get their dead into the ground fast. I dressed for the funeral in a black wool suit I had removed from the wardrobe of the best friend I ever had after *he* was murdered, having sensed at the time that from then on, whenever I mourned I would also be mourning Buddy. Talking with Buddy once, I had called myself a God-fearing atheist, and then added it was a posture that hedged my bets. Not necessarily, he had said. Maybe you're walking the high wire of ultimate judgment without any assurance there's a safety net of forgiveness below.

The bottom tongue of the black knit tie came out longer than the top, so I pulled the knot loose and started again. The second try I got the tie right.

Rabbi Hersch's funeral service was simple and dignified, and I was moved by the exalted plainchant of the *Kaddish*. My ignorance of my father's faith diminished me, as ignorance diminishes all that it touches. When it was over, we all filed outside where a hearse was standing at the head of a long line of taxicabs flying black ribbons from their aerials. Many of the drivers had not attended the service, and they stood talking by their cabs. Copies of the police flier describing the man who had his knife sharpened at Marty Kaplan's shop were much in evidence. Since the only form of mourning that would temper, if not assuage, the responsibility I felt was the capture of Frieda's killer, I had told Browder and Corelli about my conversation with the butcher.

The cops had printed the flier and staked out Kaplan's store. The rendering of the "kind of foreign" guy being anxiously scrutinized by the drivers was worthless. Marty Kaplan's descriptive powers were limited, and as in most police drawings, the eyes of the man wanted for questioning were mean and hard. Bad guy's eyes. But real bad guys didn't always look evil, just as the moments that tested what kind of man you were could be prosaic, understood only after it was too late and the opportunity was gone. Jessica had remembered word for word what Frieda had said on the phone. "He isn't there? Well, tell him I've got to talk to him right away." She had hung up abruptly.

I stared morosely at the rolling hills, still green in patches but rapidly browning, the shopping center with its acres of parking lots, the ticky-tacky homes on the ridge, as the cortege made its slow way toward the cemetery in Colma. The day was unusually muggy for San Francisco. At the gate to the cemetery we came to a halt. The entrance was being blocked by picketing gravediggers, who were on strike. A police major in charge of the escort talked with the pickets, and finally they moved up onto the curb to let us by. The body of the woman who had been organizing a taxi drivers' union was driven through the picket line to its last resting place.

I positioned myself at the edge of the mourners gathered into a horseshoe shape around the grave, standing well behind Rabbi Hersch. Several people spoke, including Geronimo and Wiley Nottingham, who was there to read a short proclamation from the mayor. I scrutinized the mourners one face at a time while he was reading. Arsonists are often to be found in the crowd watching their handiwork burn, so why not a killer at a funeral?

When it was over and I was trudging sadly away, Nottingham came up and fell in by my side. "She was a gutsy chick," he said.

"Yeah, she was."

"A nasty business."

We walked on in silence.

"Haven't heard from you since we had our little talk," he finally said. "I had the idea you were going to kind of touch base."

"What difference does it make now, man? The mayor's got her medallions, enough of them to save face anyway. And the rest of it, well . . ." I waved my hand back in the direction of Frieda's grave.

"You think with her dead a taxi strike is passé?"

"I think I don't give a damn, Wiley."

"I hear that. Keep it to yourself, but The Man, you know who I mean, he has a team out here doing a background check on the boss. Looking real good."

"The Man," I assumed, was the front runner for the Presidential nomination, the candidate Abigail Goodman was backing.

We were approaching the cemetery parking lot where cabs were pulling away rapidly, passing the mute, sign-bearing pickets on their way back to work.

"She let the chief know again that getting this creep is a priority."

"Your boss is certainly a woman who knows what comes first." I was bitter.

"You touchy again? I thought we worked that all out between us. Hey, Jackie asked after you the other day. He took a shine to you."

"You think he'd like a dog?"

"A dog?"

"Yeah, it was Frieda's. A real cute mutt. I've been taking care of it, but that's just a stopgap. You're right next to the woods, the Presidio, and I thought maybe Jackie would kind of like the companionship."

"That's damn considerate of you, Henry," he said huskily. "I don't know. I'll have to ask Ann. I mean, Jackie couldn't walk him or anything. But I'll get back to you on it. Tell you what, you come around for supper again. We'll let you know about the mutt. Maybe after the convention; things are pretty crazy until then."

"After the convention you'll have to send the limo for me and the dog. That's part of the deal."

He laughed.

Twenty

"The swelling's down," Jessica said. "But it's still a silly purple color." She touched my cheek lightly with her fingertips where Geronimo had tagged me. "Does it hurt?"

I shook my head impatiently and lifted my half-full glass toward Joseph to indicate another round. He was down at the far end of the long mahogany bar. The bar was so big they had had to saw it in half to fit it through the door when the bar had moved to its current location in 1934.

Joseph poured my Glenlivet. Then he turned to the cappuccino glasses he had lined up along the gutter of the bar. Every glass had a demitasse spoon in it, and all the spoons were resting at the same angle. I watched him carefully because that was better than talking about what talk could not assuage or change.

"You think we're cursed, our love is cursed, don't you?" Her lovely green eyes had dread in them.

I thought of things I could say. Don't worry, it will be okay. Or, we'll make up for it. Or, it wasn't your fault, I'm the one who should have known better. Or . . . or what? I didn't say any of them because I doubted the truth of them all.

"I lit a candle today," she said.

I took her hand. "I love you," I said from the bottom of my heart.

"Will that be enough?"

"For us, yes. It will be."

"You believe in us?"

Joseph cleared the empty glasses away, put down fresh napkins, placed my double Glenlivet and Jessica's cappuccino on the napkins, wiped the ashtray, counted out the cost from the pile of bills and change on the bar, smiled, and retreated.

"As implicitly as Joseph believes that cleanliness is next to godliness."

"That's an unusually Christian sentiment for you," Jessica said.

"Christian?"

"John Wesley."

"But, sweetheart, your Wesley is a Johnny-come-lately. The doctrines of religion according to the old Hebrews were carefulness, vigorousness, guiltlessness, abstemiousness, cleanliness, and godliness. Cleanliness next to godliness. Right now I fail on carefulness, guiltlessness, and abstemiousness at a minimum. Godliness isn't worth mentioning."

"How can you feel clean without guilt?" she asked.

"Damned if I know," I said, draining a large swallow of the single malt.

"Talk to me about it. Don't just brood. What ideas do you have?"

I took a deep breath. "All right. The meter in her cab wasn't running. If she had a fare, why wasn't the meter running? And why was the cab parked near her house? It was more as if she were talking to someone she knew. And why did she write 'No'?"

"Maybe she didn't," Jessica said. "Maybe whoever killed her wrote that, too. Or maybe she was trying to write a longer message and her strength gave out. The golem had *emet* written across his forehead, isn't that what you told me, but if you took a letter away the word became 'death' instead of 'truth'? There's something in that. Have you read the book the rabbi told you about?''

"No."

"You should."

"Why?"

"You just should. I don't know why. I find that my best ideas when I'm writing are always found ideas, never what I knew when I began, but what my instincts lead me toward. Isn't detecting like that, too?"

"You lit a candle?"

"Two. For her. And for us."

"You're my edge."

"And you mine. I think we may be the only two people in all of California who have never used the word 'relationship' to describe their love affair."

" 'Relationship' sounds as exciting as yesterday's meat loaf."

"The Prophet of Doom thinks he has an edge, too," Jessica said. "He thinks he's smarter than the police. He's set them clues in ancient Hebrew legends. That's his strength and that will be his weakness, too. A man's strength is usually his weakness."

A beat cop named Fallon came in from the street. He was in uniform when he walked purposefully past us, past the jukebox and the phone booth, and took a stool behind the brass cappuccino machine at the far end of the bar.

"Evening, Tom," I heard Joseph say. Fallon said nothing. Joseph poured a shot of Jameson and put it in front of him. No money changed hands. When Fallon downed the whiskey, Joseph refilled the shot glass. Fallon drank that one, too, and went back to work.

"Like him," I said. "His strength is the courage to strap on a gun and stand between us and the beasts."

"So he drinks," Jessica said. She offered me a cigarette from my own pack. When I put it between my lips she lit it and blew out the match. "All we can do is do our best."

"You really believe that? It sounds too easy."

"Do you see that we have any choice under the circumstances?"

"Vigorousness," I said, tracing a line along the underside of her wrist with my forefinger.

Her leg brushed mine. "I was hoping you'd see it that way, Hank."

Twenty-one

The Golem by Gustav Meyrink, translated into English, was listed in the card catalog on the second floor of the main library. I climbed the iron catwalk into the stacks and proceeded along the ceiling-high shelves, looking for the aisle that would contain its call number. The floor was made of translucent plastic sheets that felt unreliable underfoot. Light from the floor below glowed dully through each sheet. But for my presence among the countless millions of unspoken words, the stacks were deserted.

The slot on the shelf where *The Golem* should have been was empty. I retraced my steps past the circulation desk and down the broad central staircase. Benches set back in nooks were occupied by homeless people: one old man snoring, another clutching a book unseeingly, and a toothless woman in a smeared rag of a coat engrossed in a novel by Danielle Steel.

When I had seen that *The Golem* wasn't there I felt a plunging disappointment. Its absence made finding it and reading it seem more urgent.

I left the library and wandered across the Plaza, musing but empty-minded. Ahead of me, the dome of City Hall was lit. Though it was only just past seven on a summer night, overcast skies had turned the evening preternaturally dark. Lights were still burning in the mayor's suite; somebody was working late. It reminded me of a story about two presidential aides who were in a White House office late one evening during a crisis, watching the network news to see if the television reporters had any new information. Onto their screen came a live transmission from the lawn outside the White House. The reporter explained that the White House staff was working late, well on top of the situation. The camera panned in on the lit window of the room where the aides were watching, hoping to find out what was going on.

Old stories from reporting days. Once in Vietnam two reporters, an old hand and his young replacement, had gone out with an Army patrol when search-and-destroy was the latest strategy for winning the war. For days the reporters traveled with the patrol without seeing a single enemy combatant. On their way back to the base, the younger reporter was crestfallen. "What's the matter, my boy?" asked the older reporter. The younger man said, "I don't have any story, it's my first assignment in Vietnam, and we haven't seen a single Vietcong." "On the contrary," said the reporter who had been a while in Vietnam, "*that's* your story—not a single enemy to be seen."

That was it. I began to run back toward the library. Through two sets of doors and up the stairs past the statuelike people on the stone benches. There was a librarian at the desk, a grandmotherly-looking woman with her gray hair in an untidy bun and her reading glasses dangling from a length of black string.

"I'm looking for a book that's in the catalog but not on the shelf." I was breathing hard, as much from anxiety as from running. "*The Golem* by Gustav Meyrink. Can you tell me if it's out?"

"Just a minute," she said. She went to a computer terminal on a desk behind the counter. "Do you have the call number?" I gave it to her and she punched it into her machine.

I drummed my fingers on the countertop, dying for a cigarette.

"It's been checked out," she said, looking at her display screen. "In fact, it's quite a bit overdue."

"Checked out in January?" Aleph Mem Tof had not been written on the cab of Frank Iancini, who had been murdered before Christmas. It first showed up on Arnold Pachter's taxi in the second week of February.

"February fourth," she said. "We've sent two overdue notices. Do you want to put in a hold card?"

"It's very important that I know who has that book in his possession."

"Oh, I can't possibly give you that information. I'm sorry, we're not permitted to do that." The file was still on the screen, I could see its pale green glow but I wasn't able to read the words from where I stood. She was a nice, helpful lady and I felt bad about hopping up onto and over the counter and brushing her aside when she reached out for me. I was careful not to knock her down.

She was gutsy, too, and didn't scream but tried to get around me and wipe out the screen. I didn't stand in her way because I had what I needed. A name: Ferdinand Vegano. And an address on Crescent Avenue, out there in the Mission as Marty Kaplan had said. And if I wasn't mistaken, only two blocks away from Holly Park Circle, where Dwiri's body had been found. What had not been where it was supposed to be, that was what I had been looking for.

I had just enough presence of mind to tell the librarian I was very sorry before I dashed out to make my preparations and pick up my gun.

Twenty-two

At first light, a slash of pale pinkish orange across the fading gray of the eastern horizon, I was waiting in a taxi a hundred feet from Ferdinand Vegano's front door, on the opposite side of the street. The house was a whitewashed stucco bungalow in a row of similar houses with blank, uninviting faces crowded shoulder to shoulder. There was a security gate barring Vegano's front door. A tightly rolled advertising circular had been tossed just inside of it. Curtains were drawn across the windows on both floors. The bedroom curtain was made from a dark green bedsheet with an orange floral pattern. A sun-bleached poinsettia drooped in a plastic pot on the inside of the downstairs windowsill.

I lit a cigarette from the ember of the one I had just finished. When the pale light in the east had seeped across the sky, a newsboy pushing a handcart came around the corner, tossing bundled papers toward the doors along his route. Vegano took a *Courier*.

Lights were beginning to come on in some of the bungalows along Crescent Avenue, but there was no activity in Vegano's house. A printed notice in the window beside the faded poinsettia said: Curb Your Dog It's The Law. I was stationed almost to the corner, behind him if he walked to catch a bus or a taxi on Mission Street. To make the time pass faster, I took the window spray and a few sheets of paper towel out of the glove compartment and shined up the glass inside and out. Then, just to keep myself occupied, I wiped down the seats, front and back.

The first work-bound soul, a young woman with glossy black hair, left her house, her high heels clicking on the pavement. Somewhere nearby I heard the ponderous roar of a Sunset Scavenger truck making its rounds, and the slam and clatter of trash bins being emptied and replaced. When I looked over toward Vegano's house again there was a light behind the drawn window curtains upstairs. He was awake.

I had strapped the Walther, with a full clip in it, beneath the steering column opposite my left knee. Beside me on the front seat was an Instamatic camera. I glanced back at his lit window and nervously rubbed my palms together. They were moist.

Other people were leaving for work now, women who by their clothes and their departure hour were sales clerks, receptionists, stenographers, technicians: the first wave of workers headed toward the downtown towers and the shopping districts. Men, too, in overalls, or mismatched jackets and slacks, some carrying windbreakers or sweaters.

Two cigarettes later, after some housewives with their empty shopping carts had already set forth toward the markets, the door to Vegano's bungalow opened. I felt a jolt when I saw him, his back turned toward me while he locked his door. He was of average build, medium height, dressed in a brown polyester suit and newish shoes. There was a zippered plastic briefcase under his left arm, which he put down beside him as he worked the lock. He straightened, pocketed the keys, bent to pick up his briefcase and the newspaper. When he noticed the advertising flier that had been left on his doorstep, he picked that up, too, and put it in a trash bin, carefully replacing the lid.

He turned. A smooth, bland face, clean-shaven. Wide-set round eyes and a tawny complexion. Black hair cut very short. Some sort of Pacific Island blood, was my guess. He started toward Mission Street. I waited.

I let him get a long head start before I turned on the motor and slid slowly after him. When he was nearly to the corner of Mission, I turned on my parking lights, which activated the exterior roof lamps so that the cab was highly visible, and caught up. I reached the corner at the same time he did and pulled up at the stop sign. Marty Kaplan had said he took a lot of cabs.

Vegano glanced in my direction. His hand went into his pocket, reassuring himself that he had the cash on him that he would need. He lifted his hand. My mouth was dry and I didn't know if I could control my voice. Leaning across the front seat, I rolled down the window.

"Where you headed?"

"Downtown."

"Sure, hop in." Rolling out the welcome mat for the Prophet of Doom.

I was glad when he sat in the middle of the back seat where I had a clear view of him in the rearview, and not in the driver's side corner where I couldn't have seen him. The nape of my neck was tingling. My Adam's apple felt painfully vulnerable.

My mind was a blank, I couldn't think of anything to say, though I wanted to get him talking. I looked up and found his eyes watching me in the mirror.

"Where exactly downtown?"

"Second and Howard. Northeast corner." His voice was unaccented. "Take Folsom. You know how to do that from here?"

"Sure." It was a tricky route. I was glad it was light, since we would be passing across an uninhabited area of Bernal Hill. When I was snaking my way uphill through narrow side streets, he abruptly spoke again.

"You have a problem." My stomach lurched and my left hand jumped toward the Walther. Would I really be able to shoot him at close range, if it came to that? I had never shot anybody, never even pulled a trigger. I had not intended to play Joe Bryant's deadly possum game.

"What?" I said to the intense face in the mirror. His nose was slightly flattened.

"Your meter isn't on."

My laugh was a nervous cackle. "Jeez, I'm not awake." I hit the meter. "You get the first five blocks free, it must be your lucky day."

He didn't respond, but he never took his attention off me or where we were going.

"Most of you people don't know this way," he said.

"Don't they?" I took out a cigarette.

"I won't allow smoking."

I remembered Greg White's cigar and quietly put the cigarette aside.

"Your cab is clean," he said. "Not the usual filth. They expect you to sit in filth. The seats, the floor. Repulsive butts in the ashtrays. Your ashtrays are empty. Cleanliness is a sign of respect."

The Prophet of Doom appreciated my housecleaning. "Is it? With me, it's mostly a nervous habit."

"No. I don't think you mean that. Disrespect is the problem with America. America should be the cleanest country on earth. The filth on the buses, it's disgusting. Most taxis are sewers. The people driving them, they have no self-respect. I told one something had spilled on his back seat, it was sticky. Do you know what he said to me? He said it wasn't his problem, he sat up front. He spoke to me that way, a certified public accountant."

"It takes all kinds, I guess."

"I didn't forget. You're a Jew."

It was a word which always set my teeth on edge when it was spoken by somebody who was not Jewish himself. Jew. So lip-smacking, so blunt, so unavoidable. *A* Jew, *the* Jew:

how short a distance from the neutrality of the indefinite article to the prejudice of the definite.

"How can you tell that?"

"The Jews are the most respectful people, they respect life, they care about the suffering of the animals they slaughter out of necessity. I've made a study. Are you observant?"

"In my way. I believe a man is accountable for the things he does. For instance, if something evil happens and I'm at fault, I have to try to make up for that. But how did you get interested in Judaism?"

He stared at me without speaking. "Have you heard of the Reverend Stanley Markle?" he said.

"The fundamentalist preacher, the one on television?"

"The true man of God. He teaches that Christians must have a special affection for the State of Israel and the Jewish people. Because the Bible says that the Jews are the chosen people of God. I've made a study. The name of your God cannot be written."

"Yahweh, no."

"It can be expressed numerologically."

"Well, you're the accountant, I guess you'd know."

"A certified public accountant. In Manila. The American authorities would not recognize my license. They insisted I take a course and their licensing examination."

"So you haven't been here long?" He had round, dark eyes that bore no resemblance to the evil slits in the police circular. I met his look in the mirror, but even though he continued to talk to me, his eyes didn't engage mine. They were indwelling eyes. All they saw were the contorted depths of Ferdinand Vegano.

"Thirteen years."

"Then you've taken the exam?"

"Why should I? I'm a certified public accountant."

"But you can't practice here?"

"The time will come, they don't believe it but I know. Your meter is correct."

"Yeah."

"They cheat you. I don't forget."

"You've got some legitimate grievances there."

"No. I have no grievances. I know what is right, what is clean and what isn't. The truth is clean."

I shivered spasmodically. *Emet*. "How do you know the truth?"

"It is there to be seen."

"Not always, sometimes it's hidden. We all have our secrets, the things we don't want anybody else to know. I do. You must."

He didn't respond, but kept his eyes boring into the mirror. I kept my hand on my knee, near my gun.

"The filth and the cheating are everywhere. America should be the cleanest country on the face of the earth. There is no excuse. You keep your taxi clean, but you are not respectful."

"Why do you say that? My meter is honest, isn't it? My taxi is clean. I think you have a lot to say. I'm finding it very interesting, this talk we're having. I want to know more about your views."

Once again, he replied without responding. "If I have hired you, why do you disagree with me? Where would the world be if everybody disagreed with who hired him?"

We were approaching his destination, I was out of time, but there was one thing I had to do before he left the taxi. "I see your point. I'm a little out of it this morning, that's why I didn't turn on the meter. I was up all night, in the darkroom. Driving a taxi is only a moonlighting job, really. I'm a photographer."

I tried to meet his eyes, but there was nothing responsive in them. So I kept talking. "Yeah, I'm doing a major piece of work now. The taxi life, a collage. Listen, I'd like to take your picture. I take all my most interesting passengers."

I pulled up at Second and Howard. As he began to take out his money to pay me, I picked up the Instamatic and snapped a close-up of his face.

As he left the cab he said, "You are not fooling me. I can see the truth."

I watched as he went into a small office building belonging to an international shipping firm. Vegano's was that psychopathic fervor which sees some unbearably filthy truth about himself in the mirror and smashes the glass. I remembered having thought about myself that at least cleanliness did nobody else any harm.

Twenty-three

It took fifteen minutes in rush-hour traffic to reach Kaplan's Kosher Meats. The door was locked and a sign said the shop opened at nine-thirty, but I saw the freckled butcher setting up for the day's trade. I rapped on the glass. He came over, wiping his hands on his apron, and unlocked the door.

"Marty here?"

"You're the one who sent the cops around. The Prophet of Doom thing."

"Yes."

"I don't think you're very popular with Marty."

"Is he here?"

He jerked his head toward the door to the back room. It swung on flexible hinges under my hand. Marty Kaplan was running a flank of beef through an electric saw. Bits of gristle and fat flew off the whirring blade. I walked around to where he could see me.

He looked up, gave me a nasty stare, and hit a switch that shut off the motor. The sudden silence was loud.

"You lied to me. What do you want now?"

"I'm sorry, Marty. Look, is this the guy?" I held out the glossy snapshot of Ferdinand Vegano.

He took it reluctantly, holding it gingerly in two thick, red fingers, as if it might hurt him.

"Shit," he said.

Twenty-four

    Miss Lipschultz glanced up when I came through the door of the Homicide Division. Her hands remained poised over the keys of her typewriter, an emery board within easy reach.

"He said if you came in you could go right back." She was typing again before I had taken a step.

Browder was at a typewriter, too, pecking out a report one letter at a time. Corelli had his feet up on his desk. He was reading a paperback guide for the small investor.

"Well?" Browder said. Corelli laid down his book.

I took out the snapshot and handed it to Browder. "Ferdinand Vegano, certified public accountant manqué. Kaplan says he's the one who came in to have his knife sharpened." Browder took the snapshot and looked from it to Corelli, who picked up the phone and asked for Communications.

"There's more." I told him about Rabbi Loew of Prague and the legend of the golem, ending with what I had learned at the library. When I finished, Browder shot an inquiring look at his partner.

"They'll call," Corelli said.

"Why did you think I was coming up here?" I asked Browder.

"A little fairy told us," Corelli said.

"The stakeout at the butcher, they told us you were out

there talking to Kaplan and left in a hurry. We got them checking out your story with him now.''

The phone on Corelli's desk rang. He listened a minute and then nodded at Browder. ''Yeah, okay, you better get him down here. We're going to need a statement.'' To Browder he said, ''I'll run a check on this Vegano.'' He dialed a three-digit number.

Browder asked me, ''You know where he is now?''

I named the shipping firm where he worked. ''I took him down there in a taxi an hour ago.''

''Oh, Jesus Mary and Joseph, you dipshit Henry,'' Corelli said. ''If you fucked our case I'll have your nuts for pigeon soup.''

''Did he say anything to you?'' Browder asked me.

''Yeah. 'The truth is clean.' ''

''Dominic, maybe we better get Starr over here. Who's sitting?'' Morton Starr was the deputy district attorney in charge of homicide prosecutions.

Corelli said, ''Starr'll know.'' He picked up his phone again.

Browder left me there and went across the division room toward the cubicle of Warren Podesta, the commander of the Homicide Division. A moment later they emerged together, Podesta slipping into his suit jacket, and went out. Corelli picked up his book again. His lips moved when he read. Ten minutes later Browder came back alone, at almost the same moment Morton Starr showed up. On our way to the chief's office Browder filled in Starr.

''How long to get a search warrant for the home, Mort?''

Starr checked his watch. ''We can catch Lacy McGuire when she adjourns for lunch. You know the routine, an hour tops. You run a background?''

''Nothing. Clean.''

We all filed into Alphonso Riley's office, where Podesta was waiting with the chief, who had a red paper poppy in his lapel, proof that he had contributed to the Veterans of Foreign

Wars fund drive. Soon the paper poppy would be replaced by an American flag for the Fourth of July. The ostentatious patriot had a heavy, avuncular face and silver hair combed straight back from his forehead and temples. They said that the mayor's grown children called him "Uncle Alf."

When we were all seated, Podesta said, "Go ahead, Henry."

I told my story. As I talked, Browder passed the picture of Ferdinand Vegano across the desk to the chief, who studied it.

"Well?" Riley said when I had finished.

"We'd like to go for a search warrant at the house," Podesta said. "The knife, and that book. The butcher's on his way in to give a statement. There's already men watching the house and where he works."

Riley's hard blue eyes shifted to Morton Starr.

"It's enough," the prosecutor said.

"No arrest?"

"Since he's out of the house, we can presume for the day, we'd be on firmer footing if we found the knife first. We can't be too careful on this one, Chief."

Riley fixed me with the cold eyes in the kindly face. "We owe you a debt of gratitude," he said. To the room at large he added, "Thank you. Good work." Everybody stood.

"Sir," said Browder, "Henry'd maybe like to come along on the search." I hadn't said anything to him, but he was right. Relief and satisfaction were already being eroded by frustration as I watched my work slipping away into the procedural imperatives of the legal machinery.

"Morton?" the chief inquired.

"He'd have to be listed on the warrant. One, no standing. Two, he could be called at the trial."

"No," Riley said. When you came right down to it, he was paid $100,000 a year for saying yes or no. "I don't have to tell you men, all press statements will come through this office. I'd like you to respect that, too," he said to me.

The credit-grabbing had already begun. I saluted.

As we were passing his secretary's desk on our way out, the intercom buzzed. "The mayor, yes, sir," the secretary said. "I'll get her right away."

Browder jammed his hands into his pants pockets and stared at the floor.

That evening I turned on the news and watched the mayor announce the arrest of a suspect in the Prophet of Doom murders, name withheld. She was flanked by Riley, Podesta, and Wiley Nottingham.

"I want to express the gratitude of all the people of San Francisco to Chief Riley for the fine police work that has today resulted in an arrest," she said into the camera. "I'm proud of our police force. Everybody in this city of ours knows they can sleep safe in their beds. San Francisco is a special city with a police force known and respected around the world, as I have found in my travels." I turned the set off.

A while later my phone rang. I let it. Then I remembered what had happened the last time I ignored a phone call.

"You watch the press conference?" Browder.

"Yep."

"What can I tell ya, that's just the way it is. I thought you'd want to know, it was all there in the house. The knife. That book. He's the perpetrator, all right. The lab is coming up with some solid findings. You'll like this—he kept a record in his home computer, he rated every taxi ride he ever took. For—let's see here—courtesy, honesty, knowledge, and cleanliness. You should see this thing, it's bent. How much was on the meter. Tables comparing companies, daytime versus nighttime. It's unreal. Listen to this. 'Driver took Hyde Street. Jones a block shorter. Another one who thinks I'm a fool. Dirt under fingernails.' "

"Did Vegano talk?"

"Nothing. He didn't seem surprised or anything when we

lifted him, but he's keeping his mouth shut. Wait a second."
I could hear somebody say something to him.

"Henry?"

"Yeah?"

"Corelli says to tell you you're still a jerk-off in his book."

Twenty-five

    Downtown was draped with flags and bunting, and delegates and journalists with lapel badges and plastic identicards strung around their necks roamed the streets like some kind of benign invasionary force. Every taxi I passed on my way out to the Haight was full.

The door to Frieda's flat, or what had been Frieda's flat, was ajar. When I started upstairs I smelled paint, which triggered a painful memory of my mother crying on the first night in the smaller apartment we had moved into after my father died. Smell was such a storehouse of memory and longing.

The flat was stripped and echoed with my footsteps. I found the painter in the kitchen.

"Yo," he said. "It's not for rent yet. You have to check with the agent."

"I don't want to rent it."

"You don't? People have been wandering in here all week asking."

"No. I was a friend of Frieda's, the woman who lived here. I'm looking after her dog. I was hoping to find his license and vaccination records."

"Her stuff's all in boxes back there," he said, indicating an enclosed rear porch. "I think it's being shipped to a brother or somebody. You'd have to ask the landlord. But listen, I don't know about you going through it.'' He was tall and lanky and wore his long hair in a ponytail.

"It's the dog. I can't keep it. I've got to have the papers if I'm going to find it a home."

"I don't know. Well, it's no skin off my nose, I guess." He went back to rolling the kitchen walls. I went out to the porch.

The remnants of Frieda's life were deposited in a few cardboard boxes. The furniture had evidently been disposed of already. I took a deep breath and opened the first box. Clothes. I shut it. On top of the next box was the photograph of her when she had been thin. I held it in both hands, studying it. "I'm sorry, doll," I said aloud.

Nothing in Vegano's home computer had indicated whom he had killed, and the circumstances under which Frieda had died were still troubling me. Her being parked close to home and across a driveway, as if she had been talking with somebody in the taxi. The way the meter hadn't been running. And Vegano hadn't taken his knife to be sharpened, if it had been Vegano: the unsharpened blade was consistent with the facts but inconsistent with his previous behavior. But *emet* had been written on her taxi, which meant that if somebody other than Vegano had killed Frieda, it had been somebody with inside information about the investigation. The newspapers never had published specific information about what Vegano smeared in the taxis of his victims. The trouble was, so many people had known. Cops. Some reporters. A lot of cab drivers and management. The mayor and some of her people. And whoever all those people had told.

I put the photograph aside. The box was filled with paper. Insurance and bank records. Alliance stuff. Letters. Unpaid bills. How would I ever find Malcolm's papers in a half-dozen boxes like this? Old opera programs. A copy of a back issue of *Life* magazine about the Woodstock Festival. Newspaper clippings from the same era. I picked one out at random. It was about the seizure of a building by radical students at the University of Rhode Island, including a picture. Frieda had circled herself in the picture, leaning out of a window holding up one end of a banner that read: "URI Complicity. Out Now!" Bittersweet. I opened a dog-eared manila envelope and found more clippings inside. A report of a trial in Providence. The date was in 1973. Somebody named Stephen Wagner was on trial for the destruction of draft records and a violent assault on a security guard who had surprised him as he was setting fire to the government files. The watchman, according to the story I was reading, was confined to a wheelchair as a result of a spinal injury. The clip was about the watchman's testimony. He wasn't able to positively identify the defendant as the person who had attacked him: it had been dark, and he had been knocked unconscious before he got a close look. The prosecutor had described Stephen Wagner as a man of great and deceitful charm with the ability to change personalities as circumstances demanded. "A Hyde with many Jekylls," he called him. I pulled out a second clip from the pile. This one was about Frieda's testimony at the same trial. She had at first refused to cooperate with the prosecution, but was granted immunity and faced jail if she didn't cooperate. She was identified as a leader in a militant faction of the Students for a Democratic Society, and as the girlfriend of Stephen Wagner. Court had adjourned early for her attorney and the prosecutor to confer with the judge.

I checked the date and spilled all the clips out onto the floor, where I was crouched over the boxes, looking for the next day's story. The headline was: RADICAL'S GIRLFRIEND FINGERS HIM IN ATTACK. Frieda had talked rather than go to jail herself. I riffled through the rest of the clippings. Wagner had been convicted and sentenced to six years. I thought I knew now what she had meant when she told me her fat was a kind of hiding: a hiding from herself. She had betrayed a man she loved and a cause she believed in. I had reached the bottom of the box.

The next box was more clothing, so I tried the one beside it. Books, including the compact two-volume edition of the *Oxford English Dictionary*. I laughed—half the people I knew had joined the Literary Guild to rip off the cut-rate OED and then never ordered any books. The next box was mostly diaries, all the way back to 1969, when she had probably still been in high school. I wondered how she had felt about shipping her boyfriend, and picked out the diary for 1973, turning the pages until I reached the week of the trial. She had been using a green ballpoint pen. Her handwriting was full of loops and curls, and she dotted her *i*'s with little circles.

"Carlsen"—I knew from the clips that Carlsen was her lawyer— "Carlsen says that if I refuse to testify against Steve they can lock me up for six months. Indefinitely. Six months, six months, for as long as they want every time I refuse. John Mitchell's law. I'm terrified. Why fool myself? I know what I'm going to do, don't I? Steve, I'm sorry, baby. I don't deserve to be forgiven. At least I'll take the consequences whatever comes down. Me me me, that's all I'm thinking about. I hate myself tonight."

Her plaintiveness made me sad. A children's crusade gone mad, taking victims indiscriminately. I remembered meeting her under the freeway the night Joe Bryant had killed Leroy Edwards; she had used almost the same language as in that diary entry, talking about how we all change. How she had once thought she knew what was wrong, and then that she had even thought she knew the right thing to do. "Whatever comes down, I can live with it. But I chickened out on myself." What had we been talking about that had brought her around to saying that? Joe Bryant? No. In that instant I understood. "Oh, goddammit," I said aloud. Not NO, but NOT. The squiggly little line, it had been the cross bar of a T. I looked at her diary again: that was how she did her *t*'s: the cross bar was shaped like an infinity sign.

"Any luck back there?" the painter shouted from the kitchen.

"What? Not yet."

"Don't take too long, okay? I really shouldn't have let you do it."

I was already ripping the OED out of its box, and sliding out the little drawer that held the magnifying glass. Throwing other papers aside, I found the picture where Frieda had circled herself holding the banner out of the window. There were other faces beside her, and in other windows of the building. I began to examine them under the glass, one at a time, until I found him at the other end of the banner. Ten years younger, but unmistakable. Things I had noticed without paying real attention to started to come back to me. The strange look on her face when she saw him on the steps of City Hall. Ignoring his outstretched hand when we left the mayor's office. Her saying—twice—that there was something she wanted to tell me. How evasive he was about where he came from. How I had said to her under the freeway that night that I thought he wasn't such a bad guy, and she had said, "Don't be naive," just before she got wistful.

The smell in her taxi, the sweet smell I had recognized but couldn't place, his cologne. Wiley Nottingham. Only that hadn't originally been his name, not when they had been lovers and fought the system together. Back then he had still been Stephen Wagner.

In her box with the diaries I found the one for the current year and turned to the last entries. "God help me, I still feel a thrill being next to S," she had written after she had seen him at City Hall. "Does he hate me?"

On the morning of the day she died, Frieda had written in her diary: "I probably shouldn't do this, but what choice do I really have? S called and said he wants to see me, we have to sort out our relationship and everything that's happened. I'm piss scared. The whole of the world and we both end up here like this. Why did this have to happen, because what goes around comes around? Did I come all this way to do that again? Oh, I'm so scared. Get hold of yourself, Frieda!''

No matter whether you choose to forget the past or not, the past doesn't forget you. It was Wiley who had said that to me.

I shoved everything back into the boxes and went into the kitchen. The phone was still plugged in.

''You find it?'' the painter asked.

''Yeah, everything. Listen, can I use the phone?''

He looked dubious. ''Local?''

I nodded.

''It's not my phone.'' He shrugged.

When I reached his office in City Hall, his secretary told me Mr. Nottingham was at the convention hall and wasn't expected back today. So I rang Nellie Flynn and told him the favor I needed.

Twenty-six

Nellie ordered a double vodka on the rocks, and handed me an envelope embossed with *The Courier* logo. I opened it and looked inside.

"Why three?"

"One gets you in the door. And a floor pass. The third one is the press credential, it's got your photo on it."

"My photo?" Sure enough.

"I know a gal in personnel, they still had your old employee file. It hardly cost me anything. Well," he said, raising his glass, "here's to the Prophet of Doom and all he's done for us."

After a long swallow he said, "I needed that. First one since lunch." The clock behind the bar showed three p.m. "What's the appeal of getting into the convention? You can see it better on television."

"A kind of promise to a girl."

"Oh, great. I risk my job so you can make the beast with two backs. You can't take her in on that, it's only good for you. The security's brutal."

"I promised I'd wave to her on television."

"Roberts says Abigail's odds-on." Roberts was *The Courier*'s political sage. "She's going to throw away her cane and march into history."

"What are they quoting?"

"You can get her at seven to two."

"Bet against."

"This is more than a hunch?"

I took my money out of my pocket. There was more than usual there because Mel Dropo had paid me a cash bonus—"What Big John doesn't know won't hurt us"—after Vegano was arrested. I extracted a couple of $50 bills and passed them to Nellie.

"I've got to see Manchuco anyway," he said. "I hit the double at Bay Meadows yesterday."

"You bet with Chris Manchuco?"

"You know him?"

"Here," I said. "Make it two hundred for me."

Jessica answered on the first ring.

"It's me," I said. I told her what I had found.

"I don't understand," she said. "Wouldn't the police have searched her belongings?"

"They weren't looking for connections to a lover named Steve Wagner from so many years ago. They were looking for the Prophet of Doom."

"What will you do now?"

I told her my plan.

"You feel you must do it yourself?"

"Yes."

"I love you. Be careful."

Browder twisted a paper clip between his spatula fingers. He used the round end to smooth out the edges of his brush mustache, and shot a look at Corelli.

"That's right," he said.

"Vegano didn't kill Frieda, you already knew that?"

"I just said so, didn't I? He was on a Club Med vacation in the Caribbean that whole week."

"Well?"

"Well, what?" Browder said. The furrows across his forehead smoothed out as he tried to make his face look disinterested.

Corelli smirked. "He wants to know what we're doing about it, Jim."

Browder remained silent.

"It's just a feeling, you know, but something tells me Henry here thinks he knows who did her. Whattaya say, Jimmy, is he a sharp tack or what?"

Talking to Browder, I said, "Let me tell you a story." Browder's paper clip was a straight line when I finished. "So he had motive enough. He wanted to get revenge against Frieda, of course. And she posed a threat to what he had built for himself out here if she revealed what she knew about him. Then there was the political thing, the possibility of a taxi strike during the convention and the disruptive effect that might have had on Abigail's chances, and on his own ambitions. He knew about Aleph Mem Tof. And he was capable of violence."

"Why didn't she blow the whistle on him the first time she saw him?"

"The impression I got from her diary was that she felt guilty about what she had done at the trial," I said. "And seeing him was a shock, she needed time to absorb it. I think at first her concern was justifying herself to him. You see, she was still carrying the torch for him. And maybe when they were together he charmed her into thinking all was forgiven. She was hesitating, trying to decide what it meant to her, and then she began to think—I'm just speculating now—that he would have to help her on the political stuff, the new medallions, because what she knew about him was an implied threat. The Alliance was real important to her."

Corelli jumped out of his chair. "C'mon, Jimmy, let's lift him. What are you waiting for?" The smirk was even wider.

"Evidence would be nice," Browder said, as I expected he would.

Corelli smacked his forehead. "Jeez, he forgot about that." He sat back down, shaking his head.

"There's enough to question him, and to get a search warrant for his place."

"He works for the mayor," Browder said. "We couldn't do it on our own hook, even if we had any hard proof."

"So you won't bring him in?" I tried to sound bitter.

"We'll work on it," Browder said.

"I can do better than that." I scowled as I stood up.

"Don't do anything stupid, Henry."

"Him? Stupid? What are you talking about, Jim? He don't even know the meaning of the word." Did Corelli know that what he had said was actually clever?

I stalked out. When I reached Miss Lipschultz I stopped. Absently I said to her, "Damn, I forgot my pen," and returned to the open door. Browder was on the phone, and Corelli was shrugging on his jacket. They were getting ready to come after me, which was what I wanted. I needed them to be present for what I intended to do to work. I stopped, patted my pocket, and reversed direction.

"Dumb of me," I told Miss Lipschultz. "It was right here." I needn't have bothered with the elaborate byplay. She never looked up from her *Cosmopolitan*.

"Good," she said.

Twenty-seven

The upper lobby of the Moscone Center was jammed with milling, smoking, talking humanity. I took the down escalator. My stomach was hollow, and made a sudden watery rumble, part fear and part emptiness. I hadn't eaten.

Neatly dressed, earnest-looking boys and girls were hurrying this way and that, carrying messages, while delegates were ceaselessly moving into and out of the hall. Each time the doors swung open a roar of sound reached me, and a glimpse of people massed in a dark, crowded cavern stabbed by beams of smoky light. I went through the doors. The huge hall was hot and tight, with an odor that brought back visits to the circus. I had to move crabwise through some areas, the human traffic was that dense.

High above the people on the convention floor was an elongated podium, a podium Orson Welles might have imagined for a movie about a dictator. The head and shoulders of a man making a speech were just visible above the podium. Suspended behind him were two giant screens on which his face appeared in gargantuan close-up. The color was washed out. It was a familiar face, the face of a United States senator.

"Mah friends," the pampered face with its habitual expression of false sincerity was saying, his voice amplified through speaker clusters hanging from the ceiling, "the party of FDR, the party of JFK, the party of LBJ, the party of all people big and small, the party that has always stood for compassion, justice, *and* equality, our party, the party of the people of this great land, the party which is going to be the first to nominate and *elect* a woman to the exalted office of Vice President of the United States . . ." He was drowned out by thunderous applause. I looked up and saw the illuminated booths of the television networks, suspended like flying house trailers with picture windows. "The whole world is watching": how long ago that seemed, that sickening, stirring convention in Chicago.

The senator, made tiny by the size and height of his podium, and simultaneously made bigger than life by modern technology, boomed out the name of a nominee, the one to whom Abigail Goodman had hitched her star. Rehearsed pandemonium embroiled the arena. A brass band began to play "Happy Days Are Here Again," balloons filled the air, delegates began to march and conga through the aisles, waving placards and straw boaters with red, white, and blue bands. The din and the commotion were overwhelming. I pressed forward, looking for one man for whom all this was a rite of personal triumph so desperately desired that he had murdered rather than risk losing his moment. A man whose nerves must be stretched taut as a trip wire, over which, I thought, I could push him to his fall by the shock of his secret being discovered.

The California delegation was near the front of the hall, to the right of the podium. I moved in that direction as best as I could in the chaos. The conga line showed no sign of disbanding, but many delegates remained in or near their chairs, talking, reading newspapers; one was even watching the demonstration around him on a portable television. The senator had stepped back from the podium and was talking to somebody behind him. The camera trailed him. On the big screens I saw dignitaries and staff who were out of sight from the floor. The camera caught Abigail smiling and nodding at the governor of New York. And walking toward her was Wiley Nottingham. He reached her and bent over to say something. She shifted her weight on her cane and leaned toward him. The camera moved on. So did I.

At the foot of the steps which led up to the podium I was stopped by two men, both of them lean and one suntanned. They had buttons in their lapels, silver pens in their outside breast pockets, and tiny microphones plugged into their ears.

"Press not allowed up there," one of them said, reading my dog tags. The other shifted his weight onto the balls of his feet, though he wasn't looking at me. I looked up at the steps, carpeted in red. Wiley Nottingham was descending. When he saw me, he winked. I remembered him standing over Frieda's grave reading a proclamation from the mayor, and began to tremble with fury.

When he was a few steps above me, I leaned up and said into his ear, "She still loved you, Steve. And you killed her." I could smell his cologne.

He stopped. His face, which had been smiling and full of the color of excitement and good health, turned gray and his cheeks sank inward.

"No," he said. "How . . . she was going to . . ." Then he gained some modicum of self-control, shook his head as if clearing it, and started to climb the steps again.

I shouted, "The whole world is watching again, Steve. You slit her throat, Steve." The Secret Service agents moved toward me, but I spun and started moving away, fast.

As I passed beneath the press stand I yelled and pointed until I saw I had the attention of a few reporters. I kept moving, not sure of exactly where I was headed but trying to work my way around toward the rear of the platform. I was shoving people out of my way, leaving a ripple of shock, anger, and curiosity behind me. I passed out of the hall through another set of doors and found myself in a long corridor with concrete walls. I started running. People I passed stopped to stare. I heard footsteps behind me, a lot of them, and, glancing back, saw men and women trotting along, their dog tags swinging. Long live pack journalism! I ran faster when I saw one of the agents from the podium steps talking into a walkie-talkie as he pursued me.

I turned a corner and faced a set of sliding glass doors. On the far side coming toward me walking fast was Wiley Nottingham. He was looking down at the floor and didn't see me at first. We reached the doors at almost the same instant, and our eyes met through the glass. I reached for the door handle but there wasn't one: the doors were automatically operated by pressure-triggered devices beneath the rubber carpets we were standing on, and they were malfunctioning. Wiley's face was drawn into a mask of fearsome loathing and fright. The flesh pulled tight over his skull was taut, grayish, and blotchy. Very deliberately, I lifted my hand and drew two fingers across my throat. He bared his teeth in what looked like a savagely deranged smile. Was that horrific face the last thing Frieda had seen before she died?

With a spasmodic jerk, the stalled doors lurched open between us. He reacted more quickly than I did, stepping forward, planting his foot with his knee bent, and launching a blow with the base of his palm that caught me just below the ear. "Jackie," he howled.

As I was falling I heard somebody scream, and a man's voice shout, "What the hell?" As everything went spiraling away from me I saw the image of his wheelchair-bound boy, Jackie.

I don't know how long it was before I came to, but as soon as I opened my eyes I wished I hadn't. I seemed to be on my back, and there was a stabbingly bright light shining into my eyes, pulverizing my whole head with pain. I almost passed out again.

A familiar voice said, "The tough guy's coming around, Jim. His little tucky-bye is all over."

Without reopening my eyes I extended a hand upward. "My name is Benjamin Disraeli Henry. Will you kiss me, Corelli? I love you, too."

Twenty-eight

You could tell autumn was upon us. There was a suggestion of the cold, fresh smell of snow in the clear, crisp air, though in San Francisco the suggestion never went any further than that. As I walked along California Street past the private club in the old Flood Mansion, the only surviving residence of the nabobs whose baronial homes had given Nob Hill its name, a cable car spruced up with a fresh coat of paint for the convention dingalinged past packed with rubbernecking tourists.

I felt invigorated, better than I had felt at any time since the day I had gone with Nellie Flynn to Chris Manchuco to collect on my bet against Abigail. He had paid in crisp new bills, and I had used the money to buy Jessica and me plane tickets to Isla Mujeres, off the coast of Yucatán. Our first day there, sipping cool drinks in the shade of a beach umbrella beneath an equatorial sun, she had said, "It's a dangerous illusion, don't you think, that there's such a thing as a fresh start. It's part of what makes California fascinating and foreign. Ferdinand Vegano was a victim of the illusion, and so was Wiley Nottingham. Maybe we are, too, and refuse to see it."

"We've earned our forgiveness," I said, wanting it to be true.

"Do you believe that? Are things ever so simple? It's love that's making me wound Michael."

163

"The trouble is," I said, "that we don't want to have any secrets from ourselves."

"But we also know that there are nothing but secrets," she said, taking my hand.

We had flown out of San Francisco the same week Wiley had been indicted for Frieda's murder. His ranting tirade as he tried to strangle me with fifty reporters looking on, his arrest, and the stories that broke had effectively dashed Abigail's chances of being Vice President. Kook City had done her in just the way Wiley had worried it would.

Yet if Abigail hadn't lost her chance to make history, I would not have been on Nob Hill on this fine morning touched by an intimation of the changing seasons. Today the mayor of San Francisco, accompanied by the archbishop, a short, balding man with a round, red nose, was in the forecourt of the Mark Hopkins Hotel to bless the fleet—the taxi fleet. It was a photo opportunity not to be missed.

A Dixieland combo was belting out, "San Francisco, open your Golden Gate"—had the songwriter thought the Golden Gate was a drawbridge?—and a line of taxis with their motors belching exhaust fumes was waiting to receive their just rewards from God and government, a free Continental breakfast consisting of a soggy croissant, reconstituted orange drink, and coffee with nondairy creamer. The mayor was leaning on her cane, smiling her public smile. She was dressed in an emerald suit that showed off her honey hair and her green eyes.

Her hair was being whipped by the strong, clean breeze that was also lifting the bishop's shawl and making it flap. Only Action George was unflappable. As the band finished and the mayor stepped forward he made a gesture to his technician, who began to record the event that had no rhyme or reason except to be recorded by television.

"Our administration," she said, "is proud of our record in prioritizing better taxi service for all our people. We're making San Francisco a great taxicab city and we're not going to take a backseat to anyone.'' At just that moment our eyes met, and she gave me a look of glacial venom.

I turned away and went up to the doorman decked out in livery and a high hat. I palmed a $20 bill and showed it to him.

''I want to buy your umbrella.''

He never hesitated but leaned inside the front door, picked an umbrella out of a stand, and passed it to me. Then he shook my hand, the hand with the money in it. I carried the umbrella over to where the mayor was speaking and waited until she had finished her speech and the first taxi in line was pulling forward to be blessed by the bishop and collect a free breakfast.

''Madam our Mayor,'' I said loudly, offering her the umbrella. ''With the compliments of Frieda Mishkin.''

As she took it, staring daggers into my heart, Action George barked, ''That's a wrap. We got good stuff except for that clown with the umbrella at the end there.''